image comics presents

ROBERT KIRKMAN
CREATOR, WRITER

CHARLIE ADLARD
PENCILER, INKER (PAGES 149-218)

STEFANO GAUDIANO
INKER (PAGES 3-146)

CLIFF RATHBURN
GRAY TONES

RUS WOOTON
LETTERER

CHARLIE ADLARD & DAVE STEWART
COVER

SEAN MACKIEWICZ
EDITOR

THE WALKING DEAD, VOL. 32: REST IN PEACE. First Printing. ISBN: 978-1-5343-1241-8 Published by Image Comics, Inc. Office of publication: 2701 NW Vaughn St., Ste. 780, Portland, OR 97210.

I'D LIKE TO THANK YOU ALL FOR GATHERING ON SUCH SHORT NOTICE.

I WISH I WERE HERE TO DELIVER BETTER NEWS.
I THINK WE ARE ALL AWARE OF THE *TENSIONS* THAT HAVE BEEN BUILDING IN OUR COMMUNITY OVER THE LAST FEW WEEKS.
I HAVE BEEN CONCERNED THAT THINGS WERE GOING TO GET OUT OF HAND. UNFORTUNATELY, LAST NIGHT MY FEARS WERE *CONFIRMED.*

I KNOW HOW NEWS TRAVELS FAST HERE AND HOW THINGS CAN GET DISTORTED. I CALLED THIS MEETING TO AVOID THAT.

SO LET ME BE AS CLEAR AS POSSIBLE.
IN THE EARLY HOURS OF LAST EVENING, THERE WAS AN ASSASSINATION ATTEMPT...

...AND RICK GRIMES SAVED MY LIFE.

THE WOULD-BE ASSASSIN WAS DWIGHT, A MEMBER OF RICK'S GROUP. HE WAS A DISTURBED INDIVIDUAL WHO DIDN'T UNDERSTAND CERTAIN ELEMENTS OF OUR WAY OF LIFE. HIS OBSESSION WITH US FED A DARKNESS THAT WAS BREWING INSIDE OF HIM FOR SOME TIME.
I DO NOT WANT HIS ACTIONS TO BE USED AGAINST RICK OR THE REST OF HIS PEOPLE. THEY ARE STILL WELCOME HERE, AS IS ANYONE WHO WE ENCOUNTER.
TO THAT END, I HAVE ASKED RICK TO SAY A FEW WORDS.

PEOPLE OF THE COMMONWEALTH, I GIVE YOU MY SAVIOR, RICK GRIMES.

THANK YOU, GOVERNOR MILTON.
I, UH... DON'T REALLY KNOW WHAT TO SAY...

I KNOW THESE ARE DIFFICULT TIMES, EVEN PAINFUL FOR SOME. LINES ARE BEING DRAWN IN YOUR COMMUNITY, AND PEOPLE ARE STARTING TO TAKE SIDES.
BELIEVE ME WHEN I SAY I KNOW THE DANGERS THAT MAY LIE AHEAD. FOR MY PART, I PLAN TO DO WHATEVER I CAN TO HELP FIND A PEACEFUL SOLUTION TO ALL THE UNREST BREWING IN THE COMMONWEALTH.

MAGNA, YOU SENT FOR ME?

OH, SIDDIQ.
YES, I DID. PLEASE COME IN.

I NEED YOU TO GO BACK TO THE COMMONWEALTH.

WHAT? *WHY?*
I WANT TO KNOW WHAT'S GOING ON. I FEEL LIKE THEY SHOULD HAVE BEEN BACK BY NOW, AND I'M *WORRIED.*
THE PROBLEM IS I DON'T HAVE VERY MANY PEOPLE TO SPARE HERE, SO I'LL NEED YOU TO GO TO THE HILLTOP. I'M SURE MAGGIE COULD SPARE A FEW PEOPLE TO ACCOMPANY YOU.

YEAH, I CAN DO THAT, TOTALLY.
WHEN DO YOU WANT ME TO LEAVE?

RIGHT NOW.

WHAT ARE YOU DOING HERE?

SORRY, I, UM, LEFT SOME THINGS HERE AND NEEDED TO GET THEM BACK. I TOTALLY BROKE IN. I DON'T MEAN TO GLOSS OVER THAT. SORRY.
I HOPE YOU UNDERSTAND.
YOU'RE LEAVING THE COMMON-WEALTH?

YEAH, LOOK, I DON'T DO SO WELL WHEN THINGS GET UGLY, AND WITH EVERYTHING GOING ON, IT'S PRETTY CLEAR THINGS ARE GOING TO BE UGLY HERE FOR A WHILE.
SO I REALLY NEED TO NOT BE HERE.

FAIR ENOUGH. I KIND OF FEEL LIKE I DESERVE A BETTER EXPLANATION THAN THAT, BUT FAIR ENOUGH.

SIGH.
SIT DOWN.

I HAVE HAD A HARD LIFE.
YEAH, I KNOW. "WHO HASN'T?" RIGHT?
BUT I MEAN BEFORE ALL THIS.

MY DAD LEFT WHEN I WAS YOUNG... WHICH SUCKED... A LOT. LATER, WHEN I WAS TEN, MY MOM REMARRIED, AND THE GUY BROUGHT MY EVIL STEP-BROTHER WITH HIM.
HE WAS PRETTY MUCH AN ADULT ALREADY... SO SUDDENLY THERE WERE THESE TWO MEN JUST MOVING IN WITH MY MOM AND ME.
THINGS GOT WORSE FROM THERE.

I WASN'T WHAT YOU'D CALL A MODEL CHILD... I ACTED UP, ACTED OUT. YOU NAME IT, I DID IT. HAVING A NEW STEPDAD WITH ALL KINDS OF NEW, MESSED-UP RULES DIDN'T HELP.
I GOT PUNISHED A LOT.

BUT NOT YOUR TYPICAL...
THEY WORKED TOGETHER, MY NEW STEPFAMILY, BOTH OF THEM...THEY'D TIE ME UP, LOCK ME IN A... CLOSET.

THEY'D LEAVE ME THERE FOR HOURS... SOMETIMES... I'D PEE MY PANTS...
THAT'D JUST MAKE THEM MORE MAD...

THEY'D TAKE TURNS BEATING ME... WHEN ONE GOT TIRED, THE OTHER ONE WOULD JUMP IN.

MY MOM, SHE DIDN'T SEEM TO CARE... SHE WAS JUST HAPPY SHE WASN'T ALONE ANYMORE.
I DON'T MIND BEING ALONE.
SO THAT... WAS MY LIFE... MY *WHOLE* LIFE, UNTIL ALL *THIS* HAPPENED... WHICH IS WORSE, I'LL ADMIT.

IT CHANGES THINGS, GROWING UP LIKE THAT. WHERE MOST PEOPLE SEE A MAN... I SEE AN EVIL MONSTER. LONG BEFORE MEN WERE ACTUALLY DYING AND COMING BACK AS EVIL MONSTERS.
IT WAS HARD, WITH YOU... SEEING YOU AS SOMETHING NOT EVIL... BUT IN THAT MOMENT AFTER WE'D KILLED ALL THOSE DEAD, YOU WERE A HERO.

SO... BECAUSE *THAT* WAS MY LIFE FOR *SO* LONG... I DON'T LET DARKNESS INTO MY LIFE IF I CAN HELP IT.
THAT'S WHY I TRY TO BE SO CHEERFUL... IF I'M HAPPY, IT SEEMS TO MAKE OTHERS CHILL OUT A LITTLE AND... BE HAPPY.

THAT'S WHY I CAN'T BE HERE FOR THIS. IF THINGS GET BAD... OR SEEM LIKE THEY'RE GOING TO BE BAD... I'M NOT LIKE MY MOM.
I'D RATHER JUST BE **ALONE.**

SO... YOU'RE *LEAVING?*

I AM.
ANYTHING I COULD DO TO TALK YOU OUT OF IT?

I DON'T THINK SO.
NO. I'M SORRY.
YOU WERE NICE, BUT... NO.

PRETTY MUCH. I BARELY REMEMBER MY REAL MOTHER AT THIS POINT. WELL, THAT'S NOT FAIR TO SAY. I REMEMBER HER, BUT ALL THOSE MEMORIES ARE TIED INTO SO MUCH PAIN THAT I SORT OF BLOCK THEM OUT.
SO YEAH, MAGGIE'S BEEN A MOTHER TO ME FOR WHAT SEEMS LIKE MOST OF MY LIFE... ALL THE PARTS I CARE TO REMEMBER, AT LEAST.

YEAH, THAT'S COOL. I CAN'T BELIEVE YOUR MOM IS THE ONE WHO RUNS THIS WHOLE PLACE.

SORRY, I DIDN'T MEAN TO BRING UP MY SAD MEMORIES. NOT EXACTLY GREAT FIRST DATE CONVERSATION.

ARE YOU KIDDING? MY PARENTS AND I HAVE BEEN ON THE ROAD BY OURSELVES FOR THE PAST TWO YEARS. BEFORE WE GOT HERE, WE WERE SO DESPERATE, WE WERE GOING TO LIVE WITH PEOPLE WHO WORE SKIN AS MASKS.
IF WE DON'T TALK ABOUT SAD MEMORIES, WHAT *ELSE* IS THERE TO TALK ABOUT?

WELL, AIN'T THAT THE TRUTH.

SO TELL ME THEN, WHAT KIND OF HORRIBLE SHIT HAPPENED TO YOU BEFORE YOU AND YOUR PARENTS GOT HERE?

WHAT'S GOT YOU SMILING LIKE THAT?
IT'S SOPHIA.

OH YEAH? SOPHIA MAKES YOU HAPPY NOW?
WHAT?! NO. NOT LIKE THAT.
THAT'S NOT WHAT I MEANT.

SHE'S BEEN REALLY LONELY LATELY. BUT SHE'S ON A DATE WITH THAT NEW KID--JOSH. THEY SEEM TO BE HAVING A GOOD TIME.
I'M HAPPY FOR HER.

YOU LOVE HER, DON'T YOU?

YEAH. I DO. AS A FRIEND.
PLEASE, LYDIA... DON'T MISUNDERSTAND. WHAT I HAVE WITH YOU... IT'S DIFFERENT.

IT'S SPECIAL.
IT IS?

SOPHIA AND I GREW UP TOGETHER. SOME OF MY OLDEST MEMORIES ARE PLAYING WITH HER... HIDING WITH HER.
THERE'S A BOND THERE I CAN'T DENY... BUT IT'S **FRIENDSHIP.** OKAY?

WHAT YOU AND I HAVE... I COULD NEVER HAVE THAT WITH SOPHIA. THERE'S A DARKNESS IN ME THAT I KNOW IS THERE. I KNOW THE THINGS I'VE DONE...
...THE LIVES I'VE TAKEN... THE PAIN I'VE CAUSED. I'VE HAD TO DO TERRIBLE THINGS TO GET BY. SAME AS YOU.
I LOOK AT YOU, AND I SEE WHAT YOU'VE DONE, BUT I DON'T CARE... I SEE THE **GOOD** IN YOU INSTEAD. SAME WITH ME. YOU KNOW WHO I AM, WHAT I'VE DONE... YOU STILL SEE... **ME.**

THERE'S AN **UNDERSTANDING** BETWEEN US... BECAUSE...
...WE'RE **BOTH** MONSTERS.

YOU THINK I'M A...
...**MONSTER?**

LYDIA, PLEASE.

SLAM!

SHUKK!

SHUKK!

SHAKK!

BLAM!

EVERYTHING OKAY, MERCER?
HUFF.
HUFF.
HUFF.

WHAT DO YOU WANT?

I KNOW WE DON'T KNOW EACH OTHER, BUT I CAN'T HELP BUT NOTICE IT LOOKS LIKE YOU'VE GOT A LOT OF STEAM TO BLOW OFF...

WHAT?

IF YOU'RE PISSED OFF ABOUT HOW FUCKED UP THINGS HAVE GOTTEN AROUND HERE, THEN IT WOULD SEEM WE'RE BOTH FRUSTRATED BY THE SAME THING.
ANY INTEREST IN PUTTING THAT FRUSTRATION TO GOOD USE?

...
MAYBE.

I KNOW IT'S NOT ENOUGH, BUT I'M SORRY.
I MADE A **MISTAKE.** I WANT YOU TO KNOW THAT I KNOW THAT.

THAT'S NOT GOING TO BRING DWIGHT BACK THOUGH, *IS IT?*

CAN I SIT?
I'M SITTING DOWN.

I CREATED A BAD SITUATION. THAT MUCH IS TRUE. BUT YOU CAN'T PIN DWIGHT'S ACTIONS ON ME, OR AT LEAST YOU ***SHOULDN'T.***
THAT MAN WAS A LOOSE CANNON TO SAY THE LEAST. HE HAD ALREADY FLOWN OFF THE HANDLE THE DAY BEFORE. THINGS JUST KEPT ***ESCALATING*** WITH HIM.
I SEEM TO RECALL NOT TOO LONG AGO WHEN YOU WERE ON THE OTHER SIDE OF HIS GUN. SO I'M SAYING I SENSE A ***PATTERN,*** AND I WASN'T A HUGE PART OF IT.

I'M SORRY.

WHAT? I COULDN'T QUITE HEAR THAT.

A MAN IS DEAD, MICHONNE.

AND I'M SAYING THAT WAS *INEVITABLE.*
THAT GUY WAS **FAR** BEYOND HIS THIRD STRIKE.

I CAME TO THIS TABLE TO REMIND ME OF HOW DIFFERENT THINGS ARE, HOW FAR THESE PEOPLE HAVE COME, AND HOW MUCH IS AT STAKE.
WE'VE ENCOUNTERED NEW PEOPLE AND MOVED TO NEW PLACES BEFORE, AND THAT'S BROUGHT CONFLICT, BUT THERE'S NEVER BEEN **ANYTHING** LIKE THIS.
SO IF I SEEM LIKE I'M PUSHING **TOO HARD** OR IF I'M NOT MYSELF, IT'S BECAUSE I ALREADY FEEL THE WEIGHT OF THIS PLACE ON MY SHOULDERS. I DON'T WANT TO SCREW UP WHAT THEY HAVE HERE.
IF WE COULD MAKE THINGS WORK HERE, THEN WE'RE ON THE ROAD BACK TO NORMAL.

OKAY, ALL OF THAT RIGHT BACK AT YOU...
...BECAUSE I THINK YOU'RE **RIGHT.**

I'M JUST SAYING, IF DANTE CAN LAND A WOMAN LIKE MAGGIE, IT GIVES ME HOPE.
HEY, WHAT'S--

STOP RIGHT THERE!

EDUARDO?! IT'S ME! IT'S SIDDIQ!
I SIGNALED BEFORE I APPROACHED. WEREN'T YOU LOOKING?!

YEAH.
SORRY, MAN. COME ON IN.

WHAT THE HELL, MAN? I THOUGHT YOU WERE LOOKING.
I DON'T KNOW. THINGS HAVE BEEN SO QUIET LATELY... I GUESS I'M OFF MY GAME.

I AGREE WITH MAGNA. I'M VERY WORRIED THAT I HAVEN'T HEARD ANYTHING FROM RICK SINCE HE WENT TO THE COMMONWEALTH, SO I'D LIKE TO ASK SOME OF YOU TO ACCOMPANY SIDDIQ ON HIS TRIP.
I DON'T KNOW WHAT I'LL BE SENDING YOU INTO, SO I'M MAKING THIS COMPLETELY VOLUNTARY. IF ANY OF YOU ARE WILLING TO--

I'D LIKE TO--

YEAH, UH--
WE'D LIKE TO GO.

I'VE SPENT MY FAIR SHARE OF DAYS BEYOND THE WALL. I FEEL LIKE I'D BE USEFUL OUT THERE, SO I'D ALSO LIKE TO VOLUNTEER MY SERVICES.
THAT IS, OF COURSE, IF YOU CAN STAND TO BE AWAY FROM ME.

SOMEHOW I'LL MANAGE.

HARSH.

SIDDIQ, YOU KNOW THE LAYOUT OF THE COMMONWEALTH AND THEIR SECURITY. IS IT POSSIBLE TO OBSERVE THEM FROM A SAFE DISTANCE?
I'M JUST HOPING WE CAN KEEP THIS AS SIMPLE AS POSSIBLE.

THEY'RE A PRETTY OPEN SETTLEMENT. IF THAT'S SUDDENLY CHANGED, WE'LL KNOW SOMETHING IS UP.

OKAY, THEN. THAT'S THE PLAN. RIDE UP, TAKE A LOOK. IF THINGS LOOK OKAY, CHECK IN. IF THINGS HAVE GONE BAD, GET BACK HERE IN A HURRY.
KEEP IT SIMPLE.

OKAY, COOL.
LET'S GET STARTED ON OUR GOODBYES.

TAKE CARE OF YOURSELF OUT THERE.
IT'LL BE MY **NUMBER ONE** PRIORITY.

IF THERE'S ANY CHANCE MY DAD'S IN TROUBLE, I'M GOING.
THAT'S ALL THERE IS TO IT.

IF YOUR DAD IS IN TROUBLE, THE LAST THING HE WOULD WANT ME TO DO IS SEND YOU INTO THAT TROUBLE.
I REALLY THINK YOU SHOULD STAY HERE.

UNLESS YOU'RE GOING TO TIE ME UP AND LOCK ME AWAY, I'M GOING.
SO, ARE YOU GOING TO TIE ME UP?

NO.

YOU'RE LEAVING?
I AM.

OKAY.

LYDIA, WAIT--

YOU LOOKED AT ME... YOU WERE THE ONLY ONE WHO COULD LOOK AT ME. YOU'RE THE REASON I STOPPED HIDING MY INJURY. THE REASON EVERYONE CAN LOOK AT IT NOW.
YOU GAVE ME THE CONFIDENCE TO BE MYSELF.
AFTER EVERYTHING WE'VE BOTH DONE, WHAT WE'VE BECOME IN ORDER TO SURVIVE... I DON'T KNOW, YEAH... I SOMETIMES WORRY PEOPLE SEE US AS MONSTERS.
BUT WE'RE MONSTERS WHO SEE THROUGH THE UGLINESS IN EACH OTHER... AND SEE WHO WE BOTH REALLY ARE... AND THAT... MAKES ME FEEL NORMAL.

I'LL HAPPILY BE THAT KIND OF MONSTER FOR YOU.

WHAT A FUCKING DAY.
SEEMS LIKE THAT'S ALL WE GET LATELY.

ANYONE HAVE A GOOD DAY TODAY?
NO? DIDN'T THINK SO.
ME NEITHER.

CAN ANY OF YOU REMEMBER YOUR LAST GOOD DAY? I KNOW WE HAVE IT GOOD HERE IN THE COMMONWEALTH... I KNOW IT'S BETTER THAN WHATEVER WE HAD BEFORE WE GOT HERE.
BUT DON'T YOU SEE HOW MUCH **BETTER** THIS PLACE COULD BE?
DAY AFTER DAY... WE SWEAT AND TOIL AND GRIND... ***WHY?***

DO ANY OF YOU **LIKE** RISKING YOUR LIVES FOR GOVERNOR MILTON AND HER FRIENDS?

I THOUGHT NOT.

SO WHY DO WE LET THEM STAY IN POWER? THEIR POWER... IS US. WE SEE THEM SITTING ON THEIR PERCH, LOOKING DOWN ON THE REST OF US.
IT DOESN'T HAVE TO BE THAT WAY. WE CAN INSTALL NEW LEADERS... BETTER LEADERS.
WE COULD DO IT QUICKLY AND PEACEFULLY. WE COULD--

OH, MERCER...

...GOVERNOR MILTON IS GOING TO BE SO DISAPPOINTED IN YOU.

SHE'S GOING TO BE A LOT MORE THAN DISAPPOINTED BY THE TIME I'M DONE.

LOOK AROUND, MERCER. YOU'RE ALREADY DONE.
I DON'T KNOW ABOUT THAT.
GEORGE?

UM...

GEORGE?!

IT'D BE A FUN FIGHT TO WATCH, BUT--
YEAH, SURRENDER IS THE WISE CHOICE HERE, OLD FRIEND.

I'M JUST WORRIED... I CAN'T SHAKE IT.

IF YOU'RE SO WORRIED, WHY DIDN'T YOU GO WITH THEM?

I COULDN'T LEAVE THIS LITTLE GUY BEHIND FOR SO LONG.
BESIDES, THERE'S STILL SO MUCH TO BE DONE.

OH, YOU THINK I CAN'T HANDLE THIS LITTLE BOOGER ON MY OWN?

IT'S NOT THAT I DON'T THINK YOU'RE QUALIFIED, BRIANNA. I DON'T WANT TO BE AWAY FROM HERSHEL FOR SO LONG... THEY COULD BE GONE A MONTH.

EXACTLY.
SO RATHER THAN SIT ON THE EDGE OF YOUR SEAT THAT WHOLE TIME--RELAX AND TRUST THOSE BOYS CAN HANDLE THE TASK YOU SENT THEM OUT TO DO.
HEAVY HANGS THE CROWN...

WHEN SHE DOESN'T TRUST HER PEOPLE.
I DON'T TRUST THAT SMILEY BITCH FROM THE COMMONWEALTH. THAT'S WHO I DON'T TRUST.
UGH... AM I JUST WASTING TIME SENDING THEM ON A SCOUTING MISSION?
SHOULD I BE ROUNDING UP ALL OUR PEOPLE AND MARCHING AN ARMY UP TO THE COMMONWEALTH RIGHT NOW?

I DON'T KNOW... BUT I KNOW IF YOU FEEL LIKE YOU SHOULD...
THEN YOU SHOULD.

...

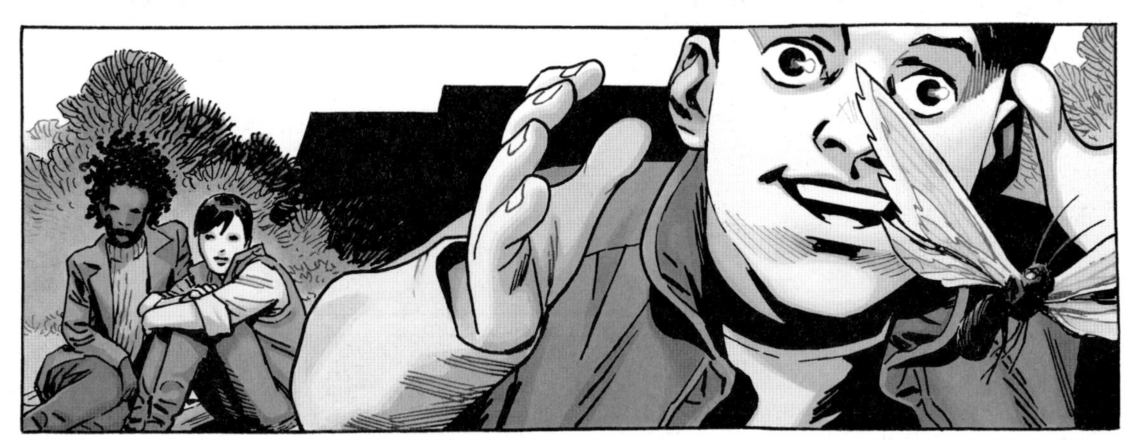

IS THAT WHAT I THINK IT IS?
I THINK IT IS.

PRINCESS?!
WHAT ARE YOU DOING OUT HERE?!

WHAT THE--?!

AFTER HER!

WHUMPP!
AAAAGH!

WHUDD!!

SHIT!
SHIT!

KRAK!

OH, SHIT!
WHAT DO WE DO?!

I GOT THIS!

WHOOM!

OH, GOD!
OH, GOD!

CARL!
JUMP!

OOF!
WHUMP!

SAVE YOURSELVES-- GO!

SVAASH!
LIKE HELL!

WE GET OUT TOGETHER OR NOT AT ALL!
FAIR ENOUGH.

RIDE ON AHEAD-- WE'LL CATCH UP!
CHRIST-- THERE'S SO MANY!

HURRY--WE GOTTA--
OH, SHIT!

SVAASH!

WE'RE NOT GOING TO OUTRUN THEM ALL ON FOOT!
WHUMP!
WHUDD!

I GOT A PLACE TO HIDE--
FOLLOW ME!

WHERE TO?
I'VE GOT A HIDING PLACE--BUT NOT FOR HORSES!

RIDE AHEAD AND FIND A GOOD PLACE TO WAIT ALONG THE ROAD--WE'LL CATCH UP.
GO!

DO THAT THING YOUR PEOPLE DO WHERE YOU RIDE YOUR HORSES AND DRIVE THE DEAD AWAY.
YOU KNOW THE THING--IT'S AWESOME!

HURRY UP-- BEFORE THEY SEE US!

I'M SO DISAPPOINTED IN YOU.

AFTER EVERYTHING WE'VE DONE FOR YOU, TAKING YOU IN, PUTTING YOU IN A POSITION OF POWER, I CAN'T BELIEVE YOU'VE TURNED ON US.
WE TRUSTED YOU, MERCER.
WHERE'S YOUR SENSE OF LOYALTY?

DID YOU SAY LOYALTY?

WHERE'S YOUR FUCKING SENSE OF LOYALTY?
I WAS NEVER MORE THAN A GLORIFIED ERRAND BOY FOR YOU. I WAS A BABYSITTER. I WAS A CHAUFFEUR. I WAS YOUR WHIPPING BOY.
YOU PUT ME IN DANGER MORE TIMES THAN I CAN REMEMBER, AND YOU NEVER SEEMED TO GIVE A FUCK ALL THE TIMES I NEARLY DIED FOR YOU.
YOU'RE NOT A LEADER, YOU'RE A FUCKING WANNABE QUEEN, AND I'M NOT WAITING AROUND UNTIL YOU TRY TO INSTALL YOUR SHIT-FOR-BRAINS SON AS YOUR REPLACEMENT.

WELL...
LOOKS LIKE YOU'RE RIGHT WHERE YOU BELONG.

WHAT'S GOING ON? CAN'T FIND THE CRESCENT WRENCH?
NO, UM, IT'S WORSE THAN THAT.

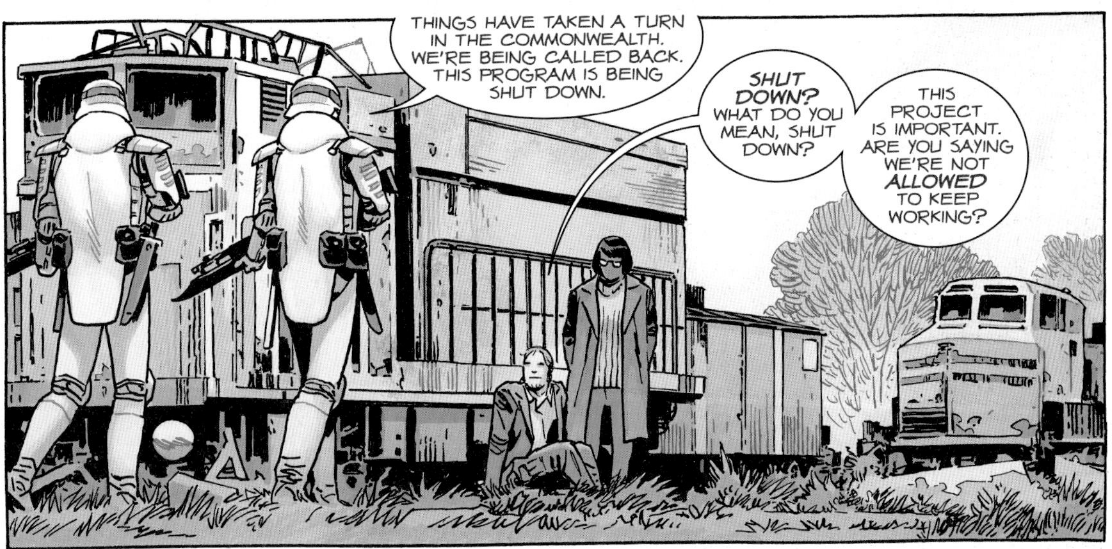
THINGS HAVE TAKEN A TURN IN THE COMMONWEALTH. WE'RE BEING CALLED BACK. THIS PROGRAM IS BEING SHUT DOWN.
SHUT DOWN? WHAT DO YOU MEAN, SHUT DOWN?
THIS PROJECT IS IMPORTANT. ARE YOU SAYING WE'RE NOT ALLOWED TO KEEP WORKING?

LOOK, MAN, I DON'T KNOW. I HAVEN'T BEEN GIVEN ORDERS TO ARREST YOU OR ANYTHING. ALL I KNOW IS MERCER IS IN JAIL AND TENSIONS ARE HIGH, AND GOVERNOR MILTON WANTS EVERYBODY TO REGROUP BACK IN TOWN.
SO WHATEVER IT IS YOU'RE DOING HERE IS NO LONGER A PRIORITY. WE CAN'T STAY HERE TO GUARD YOU. WE'VE GOTTA GO.
I MEAN, TECHNICALLY, IF IT'S THAT IMPORTANT TO YOU, YOU COULD STAY, BUT YOU WOULDN'T HAVE ANYONE HERE PROTECTING YOU.

YOU'RE NOT CONSIDERING THIS...
ARE YOU?

WELL, JUST BARGE RIGHT IN, WHY DON'T YOU?
THIS IS SERIOUS.

WHAT HAPPENED?
HOW SERIOUS?

PAMELA JUST THREW MERCER IN JAIL.

OH, GOD...

OH, GOD, IS RIGHT.

NO, YOU DON'T UNDERSTAND. THE PEOPLE ARE ALREADY ABOUT TO REVOLT. THEY DON'T TRUST THE GUARDS--BUT THEY LIKED MERCER. NOW THAT THE GUARDS HAVE TURNED AGAINST HIM--THIS IS VERY, VERY BAD.
ELODIE WAS TELLING ME THAT PEOPLE ARE ALREADY STARTING TO TAKE SIDES... THOSE WHO SUPPORT THE GOVERNOR AND THOSE WHO DON'T.

WE COULD BE ON THE CUSP OF A FULL-BLOWN CIVIL WAR WITHIN THE COMMONWEALTH.

NO, NO, NO... WE HAVE TO STOP THIS.
THIS IS WHAT DWIGHT WANTED. WHAT HE WAS WORKING TOWARD...
WHAT I DID... I DID TO *STOP* THIS.

IF IT HAPPENS *ANYWAY...*
WHAT HAVE I DONE?

DWIGHT WAS STIRRING UP THE PEOPLE-- BUT THEIR HATRED FOR GOVERNOR MILTON AND HER PEOPLE... IT'S BEEN BREWING FOR *YEARS.*
DWIGHT WAS ONLY ENCOURAGING IT--STOKING A FIRE THAT WAS ALREADY BURNING.
I WANT TO AVOID THIS AS MUCH AS YOU DO... BUT I WORRY IT'S ONLY A MATTER OF *TIME.*

NO. WE'RE A CATALYST. WE CAME--THINGS ARE GETTING WORSE. MAYBE THERE WAS RESENTMENT BREWING, BUT IT'S OUR PRESENCE THAT'S URGING THINGS ALONG.
THERE *WAS* NO ALTERNATIVE UNTIL WE SHOWED UP. *THAT'S* WHAT IT IS... THAT'S WHAT'S ACCELERATING THINGS.
I CAN'T HAVE US BE THE THING THAT TEARS THE COMMONWEALTH APART. BUT WITHOUT *DWIGHT...* HOW IS IT HAPPENING SO FAST?
WHO COULD...
WAIT.

WHERE'S *LAURA?*

BUT MERCER, MAN... I CAN'T FUCKING BELIEVE IT.
I KNOW, RIGHT?

COME ON, GEORGE. SHOOT STRAIGHT WITH ME...
WE'RE JUST BIDING TIME, RIGHT? WE'RE GOING TO GET MERCER OUT, AND WE'RE GOING TO RUN THIS SHIT.

YOU'D DO WELL TO KEEP YOUR MOUTH *SHUT.*

WHAT'S THAT ALL ABOUT?
NOTHING. SEE YOU GUYS TOMORROW.

WHO THE HELL ARE YOU?

I'M A FRIEND OF MERCER'S.
ARE YOU?

THEY'RE STARTING TO THIN OUT. SHOULD BE CLEAR IN LESS THAN AN HOUR.
AARON AND THE OTHERS MUST BE LEADING THEM AWAY. THIS IS GOOD. ONLY A MINOR DETOUR.

AND WHAT ABOUT YOU? WHAT'S HAPPENING AT THE COMMONWEALTH?
WHY ARE YOU HERE?

THINGS ARE GETTING UGLY THERE. THERE'S A LOT OF IN-FIGHTING AMONGST THE PEOPLE.
SO I LEFT.

WHAT DO YOU MEAN? IS EVERYONE OKAY-- ARE PEOPLE HURT?
HOW COULD YOU JUST LEAVE?

HOW COULD I STAY?
ONE THING I'VE LEARNED IS THAT PEOPLE ARE DANGEROUS--I KNEW THAT EVEN BEFORE. WHEN I RAN INTO YOUR PEOPLE IN PITTSBURGH, I'D BEEN ALONE FOR A LONG TIME.
HECK, I WAS DESPERATE... BUT BEING AT THE COMMONWEALTH...
IT REMINDED ME. PEOPLE AND ME... WE DON'T MIX. I'M WAY BETTER OFF ALONE.

NO YOU'RE NOT. NO ONE IS.
YOU THINK YOU'RE SOME TOUGH LONER? THAT'S A COOL IDEA AND ALL... BUT IT'S TOTAL BULLSHIT.
WHY'D YOU SAVE US THEN? YOU DIDN'T HAVE TO COME BACK. YOU RISKED YOUR LIFE... FOR US. THAT'S HOW MUCH YOU SECRETLY DON'T WANT TO BE ALONE.
PEOPLE ARE GOOD FOR YOU... AND YOU'RE GOOD FOR PEOPLE.

YOU DIDN'T HAVE TO CURSE.

THEY'RE PRETTY THINNED OUT ALREADY-- LET'S GET GOING SO WE CAN CATCH UP TO AARON AND THE REST.
WILL YOU COME WITH US?

OKAY.
YEAH.

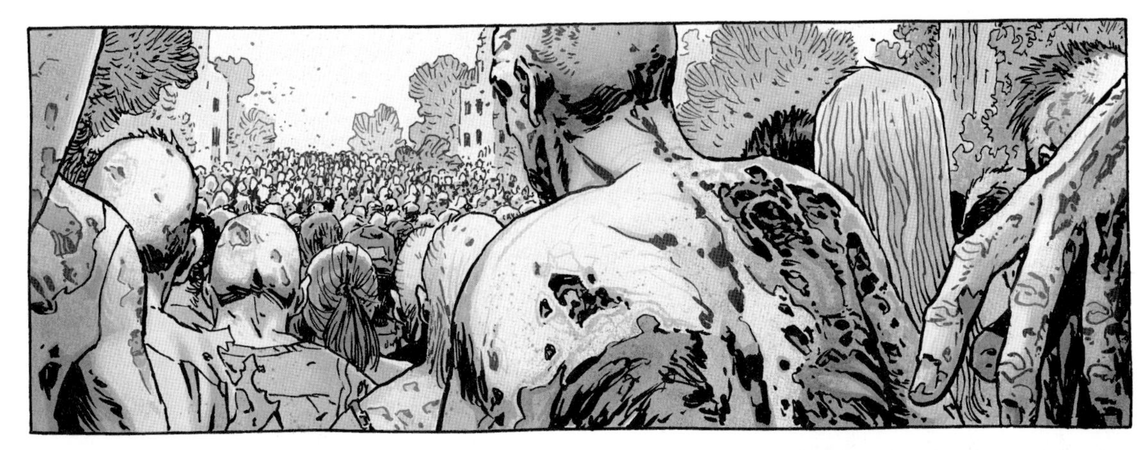

BEEN A WHILE SINCE WE'VE DEALT WITH A HERD THAT BIG...
REALLY GETS THE BLOOD PUMPING.
YEAH--AND I'VE HAD ENOUGH OF THAT. LET'S GET BACK TO THE ROAD--MEET UP WITH JESUS AND CARL.

SHUKK!

YOU KNOW, I USED TO HOPE TO GO A WHOLE *DAY* WITHOUT SAVAGELY MURDERING SOMEONE WHO USED TO BE ALIVE.
EVENTUALLY, I GOT A FREE DAY, AND THEN IT WAS A *WHOLE* WEEK THAT I WANTED. NOW... I'M PINING FOR A SOLID MONTH OF NO KILLING.
I'M JUST *GREEDY,* I GUESS.

I'VE GONE A WHOLE MONTH.
AND A YEAR, ACTUALLY.
I'M HOPING WE GET TO A POINT WHERE I'VE GOT THE WHOLE REST OF MY LIFE AHEAD OF ME... AND NOT ONE ROAMER LEFT TO KILL.

BUT FOR NOW...
HANG BACK, LOG SOME TIME OFF.

SVAASH!!
SHUKK!

YOU DIDN'T SAVE ANY FOR US.

FIGURED YOU HAD YOUR FILL.

GET UP HERE, YOU BEAUTIFUL MAN.

COME ON-- LET'S TRY AND MAKE UP SOME LOST TIME.

YOU GUYS REDIRECTED THE HERD AWAY FROM THE COMMON-WEALTH?
IT TOOK SOME DOING--BUT *YEAH.*
BEST WE COULD DO WAS SEND IT TOWARD THIS ABANDONED RAIL YARD WE FIRST MET THEM IN.
THAT SHOULD BE FAR ENOUGH AWAY.

YEAH, THAT CONNECTOR IS LOOKING PRETTY BAD. HOPEFULLY, SOME KIND OF REPLACEMENT CAN BE FOUND.
YEAH, I'M SURE WE HAVE SOMETHING THAT WOULD WORK.

WAIT, DO YOU HEAR--?
OH, GOD!

WE HAVE TO RUN!
THERE'S TOO MANY--THIS WAY!

NO, NO, NO--!

GET IN--STAY CALM!

MOVE, MOVE, MOVE!

THUNK!

THERE WERE SO-- I'VE NEVER SEEN SO MANY!
JUST LISTEN TO THEM ALL! WE'RE TRAPPED IN HERE-- TRAPPED!
WE'RE GOING TO DIE!
STEPHANIE, LISTEN. THEY'RE OUT THERE, WE'RE IN HERE. THIS ENGINE CAR IS SOLID METAL-- WE'RE SAFE.
WE'RE NOT GOING TO DIE IN HERE--

I WON'T LET US.

WELL, LOOK WHO FINALLY DECIDED TO VISIT...

TOOK ME A WHILE TO GET MY DUCKS IN A ROW. I HAD TO FIND OUT WHO YOUR FRIENDS REALLY WERE.
I KNEW GETTING YOU OUT OF HERE WOULD BE RATHER DIFFICULT, SO I NEEDED TO GET *HELP.*

THEN I'M SURPRISED YOU'RE HERE AT ALL, UNLESS IT'S JUST TO TELL ME I DON'T HAVE VERY MANY FRIENDS THESE DAYS.

YOU'D BE *SURPRISED.*
LET'S JUST SAY YOU'RE GOING TO WANT TO BE AS FAR AWAY FROM THAT BACK WALL AS POSSIBLE.

I'M NOT JUST SAYING IT-- GET AWAY FROM THAT WALL *NOW!*
WAIT-- *WHAT?!*

BRA-KOOM!

ELODIE, WAIT--!
OPEN

YOU TRYING TO KILL ME?!

OH MY GOD! OH MY GOD!
I'M SORRY!

ARE YOU OKAY?

I'LL LIVE-- IF MY EARS EVER STOP RINGING.
I'M SO SORRY. THE GUY SAID HE KNEW WHAT HE WAS DOING.

GUY?
WHAT GUY?

SORRY! I *REALLY* OVERDID IT!
WANTED TO BRING THE WALL DOWN. DAMN NEAR BROUGHT DOWN THE WHOLE PLACE.

GLAD TO SEE YOU CAME TO YOUR SENSES.
CUT ME A LITTLE SLACK, MAN. WITH LANCE THERE, I DIDN'T KNOW WHO WAS ON OUR SIDE AND WHO WASN'T.
I'D BE NO GOOD TO YOU IF I WAS IN THE CELL NEXT TO YOU.

FAIR ENOUGH.
NOW WHAT'S THE PLAN?

IT'S PRETTY SIMPLE, REALLY...

WE'RE GOING TO RALLY THE TROOPS AND LIBERATE THE PEOPLE OF THE COMMONWEALTH.

YOU HAVE TO GO!
NOW!

RICK?!
HAVE YOU LOST YOUR MIND?!

I'M TRYING TO SAVE YOU!

THIS IS OUTRAGEOUS-- SAVE ME FROM WHAT?

DON'T YOU REALIZE WHERE THE EXPLOSION CAME FROM? THAT WAS THE PRISON--AND WHO WAS IT YOU JUST PUT THERE?
THAT WAS MERCER BEING FREED--IN THE MOST BRAZEN WAY POSSIBLE! SO SOMEONE FELT CONFIDENT ENOUGH TO BE THAT BOLD.
ASK YOURSELF HOW I GOT UP HERE IN THE FIRST PLACE! WHERE ARE YOUR GUARDS?
THEY'VE TURNED AGAINST YOU!

MOM, SOMEONE IS BANGING ON THE DOOR LIKE THEY'RE TRYING TO BREAK IN--WHAT THE HELL IS GOING ON?!

I BLOCKED THE DOOR WHEN I CAME IN. THAT'S THEM. THEY'RE COMING FOR YOU.
LEAD US TO A BACK EXIT BEFORE IT'S TOO LATE!

THIS WAY.

I CAN'T BELIEVE THIS IS HAPPENING.

EXIT
JUST KEEP MOVING.

I'M NOT TAKING ANOTHER STEP UNTIL SOMEONE EXPLAINS TO ME WHAT THE FUCK IS GOING ON!
STARTING WITH WHO THE FUCK PUT YOU IN CHARGE?!

WE ARE IN THE BEGINNINGS OF A *REVOLT.* I'M TRYING TO ENSURE YOUR MOTHER MAKES IT OUT OF HERE ALIVE.
PLEASE TRY NOT TO GET IN THE WAY.

REVOLT?! NOBODY HERE HAS THE BALLS TO DEFY US--THEY KNOW THEY'D BE *NOTHING* WITHOUT US!
ONE LITTLE EXPLOSION AND THIS OLD MAN FLIES INTO A PANIC.

WRAMM!
EVERYONE FUCKING *HATES* YOU! YOUR FAMILY TAKES ADVANTAGE OF THE PEOPLE HERE! YOU TREAT THEM LIKE SHIT! AND YOU'RE THE *WORST* AMONG THEM!
BUT YOU DON'T DESERVE TO DIE FOR WHAT YOU'VE DONE!
THAT'S THE *ONLY* REASON I'M HELPING YOU!

RICK, PLEASE LET MY SON GO.

WAIT, WAIT.

WHERE'S A GOOD PLACE YOU CAN HIDE?

NOWHERE HERE. WE NEED TO GET TO GREENVILLE.
CLORIS CAN HIDE US THERE.

WHAT'S THE FASTEST WAY OUT OF TOWN?
FOLLOW ME.

UH, RICK?

WOW, LOOKS LIKE YOU REALLY MADE A MESS OF THINGS HERE.

I PROMISE I'M TRYING TO DO THE EXACT *OPPOSITE.*
IN FACT, I COULD REALLY USE YOUR HELP.

WHOA, NOT EVEN TIME FOR HELLO. MUST BE BAD.
WHATEVER IT IS, I'M HERE FOR YOU.

THESE PEOPLE ARE IN GRAVE DANGER. I NEED YOU AND AARON TO GET THEM WHERE THEY'RE GOING.
THEY KNOW THE WAY, BUT I NEED YOU GUYS TO GO ***RIGHT NOW.***
JUST... STAY WITH THEM AND WAIT FOR WORD FROM ME.

OKAY, I CAN SEE WE'RE IN A BIT OF A HURRY.
GUYS, I'M GONNA NEED YOUR HORSES. HAND THEM OVER TO THESE FINE PEOPLE SO WE CAN GET A MOVE ON.

THEY'RE STAYING-- YOU SAID EVENTUALLY THEY WOULD MOVE ON.
TOO MANY OF THEM SAW US--THEY KNOW WE'RE IN HERE.

I'VE--NEVER DONE ANYTHING LIKE THIS-- NEVER BEEN-- SURROUNDED.
I CAN'T-- GET A HOLD OF MYSELF--I'M JUST--I'M JUST--

IT'S OKAY. I HAVE AN IDEA. I'M GOING TO GET US OUT OF HERE.

WAIT-- WHAT ARE YOU DOING?

JUST TRUST ME...
PSSSSSHHHHKK!

PSSSSHHKK!

PSSSSSHHH!

WROKK!

PSSSSSSHH!

PSSSSSSSSHHHHH!

PSSSSSHHH!

PSSSSSSSHHHHH!

OKAY--THEY'RE GOING AFTER THE FIRE EXTINGUISHER--IT'S DRAWING THEM **AWAY** FROM US.
WE JUST NEED TO STAY QUIET AND **WAIT.**
IN A LITTLE WHILE, THERE WILL BE A CLEARING AROUND US--GAPS. IT WON'T BE **CLEAR,** BUT WE CAN SLIP THROUGH, AS LONG AS WE'RE **FAST** AND **QUIET.**
WE CAN GET HOME-- WE'LL BE **SAFE.** OKAY?

I DON'T KNOW IF I CAN--I'M SCARED, EUGENE.

I AM, TOO-- BUT WE'RE GOING TO DO THIS AND IT'S GOING TO WORK...
BECAUSE I'VE DONE THIS **BEFORE.**

BACK IN ALEXANDRIA-- WE'D ONLY LIVED THERE A LITTLE WHILE, AND BEFORE THAT WE'D MOVED FROM PLACE TO PLACE, ALWAYS DRIVEN OUT BY THE DEAD-- OR WORSE.
THE WALLS WERE DOWN, THE PLACE WAS OVERRUN WITH ROAMERS. WE WERE GOING TO FLEE-- EVERY BONE IN MY BODY WANTED TO JUST RUN.
BUT *RICK,* HE LED US IN AN ATTACK-- WE GROUPED TOGETHER, PROTECTED EACH OTHER, AND WE *FOUGHT BACK.*

THAT WAS THE DAY WE STOPPED RUNNING-- WHEN WE SET ROOTS IN ALEXANDRIA AND FOUGHT TO *STAY* THERE.
THAT'S THE DAY WHEN I LEARNED TO CONTROL MY FEAR--*USE* IT. IT'S STILL THERE-- BUT IT'S A TOOL, IT KEEPS ME SHARP.

THOSE UNDEAD FUCKS ARE *TERRIFYING.*
BUT THEY'RE SLOW AND, DAMN IT, THEY'RE *STUPID.*

WE CAN BEAT THEM.
TOGETHER. LIKE RICK TAUGHT ME.
YOU WITH ME?

YEAH.

GOOD. BECAUSE THAT EXTINGUISHER IS ABOUT OUT.
NOW?
NOW.

STAY CLOSE-- STAY QUIET.

GRUH.

SHUKK!

C'MON!
C'MON!

WHUDD!
WE'RE CLEAR-- RUN-- RUN!
WE HAVE TO GET OUT OF VIEW BEFORE MORE OF THEM SEE US!

YOU SHOULDN'T HAVE COME HERE.
HOW BAD IS IT?

I DON'T KNOW... IT'S BAD AND I DON'T KNOW HOW MUCH WORSE IT'S GOING TO GET.
THE PEOPLE HERE... THERE'S BEEN A TENSION BREWING FOR YEARS AND IT'S FINALLY COME TO A HEAD.

WHAT CAN I DO?

CARL... YOU DON'T NEED ME TO TELL YOU WHAT TO DO.
WHEN THE TIME COMES, YOU'LL KNOW.

WE SHOULD HEAD BACK INTO TOWN-- SEE WHAT'S WHAT.

WHERE DID YOU FIND HIM?
HIS PLACE-- UNDER HIS BED.

WHERE'S GOVERNOR MILTON?

IF I KNEW, I'D BE *WITH HER,* YOU FUCKING MORON!

GODDAMN IT, LANCE. WE NEED TO--
TYRANT!

KEEP THOSE PEOPLE *BACK!*

FASCIST!
DISPERSE *IMMEDIATELY!* GO BACK TO YOUR HOMES--OR WE WILL HAVE NO CHOICE BUT TO USE FORCE.

SKREEESH!!

MOTHER--
FUCK!

BRAKK! BRAKK!

NEXT SHOTS END YOUR LIVES--
DISPERSE!

MERCER--
WHAT ARE
YOU
DOING?

WHAT *YOU*
SHOULD BE
DOING.
I'M
TRYING
TO *HELP*
THESE
PEOPLE.

THAT
DIDN'T
LOOK
LIKE
HELP.

THE PEOPLE
DON'T TRUST ME.
THEY'RE TURNING
AGAINST US.
AFTER EVERYTHING MY GUARDS
HAVE DONE RECENTLY--THEY
THINK WE'RE STAGING SOME
KIND OF COUP, AND THAT NOW
THINGS WILL SOMEHOW
BE *WORSE*.

LOOK
AROUND
YOU--
THEY'RE
RIGHT.

...

I'M IN OVER MY HEAD HERE--I'M DROWNING.
I CAN'T DO THIS WITHOUT YOU-- I NEED YOUR HELP.
IF THEY WON'T CHOOSE ME OVER GOVERNOR MILTON-- MAYBE THEY'LL CHOOSE YOU.

...

SHE SEEMS NICE TO YOU... BECAUSE SHE IS NICE TO YOU. SHE RESPECTS YOU... SHE THINKS YOU'RE ONE OF HER PEOPLE... **THE ELITE.**
MAYBE YOU **ARE** ELITE... BUT YOU'RE NOT LIKE HER.
YOU CARE ABOUT PEOPLE. YOU'VE SEEN HOW SHE IS... THIS UNIFORM THEY MAKE US WEAR--TO HER, IT MEANS WE'RE EXPENDABLE.

AFTER THE THINGS THEY'VE MADE US DO AND SOME OF MY MEN STEPPING OUT OF LINE... THE PEOPLE HERE, THEY DON'T TRUST US.
BUT THEY DON'T WANT TO GO BACK TO THE WAY THINGS WERE. I WON'T LET THEM... **THINGS HAVE TO CHANGE.**
I KNOW YOU AGREE WITH ME.

SO TAKE CHARGE. WE'LL BACK YOU.
LEAD THESE PEOPLE THE WAY YOU LEAD YOUR PEOPLE.
MERCER... I...
I **CAN'T.**

I'VE BEEN THROUGH THESE KINDS OF THINGS BEFORE. THE PEOPLE HERE BARELY KNOW WHO I AM. I GAVE HALF A SPEECH IN FRONT OF THEM--AND IT WAS ON **BEHALF** OF GOVERNOR MILTON. MAYBE THEY'VE SEEN ME IN THE STREETS... HEARD A STORY OR TWO...
THAT'S NOT **ENOUGH.**
THINGS CAN CHANGE... BUT NOT LIKE THIS. IT'S GOING TO TAKE MORE **TIME.**

THAT'S SOMETHING WE DON'T HAVE.

OH MY GOD...
IT'S FINALLY HAPPENED.

WHAT HAPPENED? WHAT IS IT?

I BELIEVE IN THE COMMONWEALTH... BUT I SEE ITS PROBLEMS. WE ALL DO.
THERE'S ALWAYS BEEN TALK OF OVERTHROWING THE GOVERNOR... CHANGING THE RULES.

THIS HAS TO BE THAT. THAT'S WHY SHE CALLED OUR GUARDS BACK.

SO... THIS IS A GOOD THING, THEN... RIGHT?
LET'S GET INSIDE AND FIGURE THAT OUT.

ELODIE!
MA'AM!

WE NEED THESE STREETS CLEAR, MA'AM.
RETURN TO YOUR HOME IMMEDIATELY.

I'M TRYING TO FIND MY DAUGHTER.
I PROMISE I'LL GO HOME AFTER.

I'M GOING TO LOOK THE OTHER WAY--BECAUSE I APPRECIATE WHAT YOU DID.
BUT BE FAST.

KNOCK! KNOCK!
IT'S MICHONNE-- OPEN UP!

ELODIE'S INSIDE.
THIS WAY.

WHAT--
WHAT ARE YOU DOING?!

WE'RE GETTING READY TO FIGHT.

YOU'RE WHAT--?!

GIVE ME THAT!
HEY!

WHEN YOU BRING A GUN TO A FIGHT-- THAT USUALLY MEANS BULLETS WILL BE SHOOTING BACK AT YOU.
THAT MEANS YOU DIE--SOME OF YOU-- ALL OF YOU--DOESN'T MATTER... SOMEONE DIES.
I'M NOT LOSING YOU... NOT OVER THIS.

NOT ANY OF YOU!

STAY PUT! ALL OF YOU!
DON'T FUCKING LEAVE THIS APARTMENT UNTIL YOU'VE HEARD FROM ME-- OKAY?!

...
ELODIE-- YOUR MOM IS A FUCKING BADASS.

WAIT-- QUIET-- DO YOU HEAR THAT?
OH NO!

DID WE LURE THEM HERE?!
NO WAY--WE WERE QUIET--WE WEREN'T SEEN. IT MUST HAVE BEEN WHATEVER STARTED THAT FIRE.
WE HAVE TO WARN THEM--RUN!

GET HIM INSIDE--LOCK HIM UP.
YES, SIR.
LOCK ME--ARE YOU CRAZY?!

I'LL REMEMBER THIS!

LET ME SEND FOR PAMELA--WE CAN NEGOTIATE A PEACE. ALL OF THIS CAN BE WORKED OUT--YOU HAVEN'T CROSSED A LINE YET. NO ONE HAS DIED.
THERE'S STILL TIME. THERE IS.

...

RICK!

THEY WON'T LET ME THROUGH!
RICK!

EUGENE?
LET THIS MAN THROUGH!

THERE'S A HERD COMING!
THE FUCK IS A HERD?
SWARM-- IT'S A SWARM!

THERE'S A SWARM NEARBY-- HOW BIG?!
HOW CLOSE?!
HUGE-- LOOKED LIKE AT LEAST A THOUSAND-- MORE.

RIGHT AT THE EDGE OF TOWN!
HOW IS THIS POSSIBLE?! WHERE ARE THE LOOKOUTS?!
WHEN THEY LOCKED YOU UP--PAMELA PULLED ALL THE GUARDS BACK INTO TOWN FOR PROTECTION.

MOTHER-- FUCK!

CARL?!

WHERE ARE YOU GOING? WHAT'S GOING ON?
I'M TRYING TO FIGURE THAT OUT MYSELF. WHEN DID YOU GET HERE?

SIDDIQ WAS SENT TO CHECK IN ON THINGS HERE-- I TAGGED ALONG.

EXCELLENT TIMING.

MICHONNE! CARL!
COME ON, HURRY-- WE HAVE TO GET INSIDE!

WHY-- WHAT'S GOING ON?!
THERE'S A HERD COMING IN-- WE HAVE TO CLEAR THE STREETS!
LET'S GO!

I CAN'T-- I HAVE TO BE WITH ELODIE!

OKAY.
STAY SAFE.

GO WITH HER!
MAKE SURE THE STREETS ARE CLEAR AND EVERYONE IS INSIDE ON YOUR WAY!

EVERYONE KEEP QUIET AND STAY AWAY FROM THE WINDOWS. WE NEED TO STAY OUT OF VIEW. IF THEY DON'T KNOW WE'RE HERE, THEY'LL JUST PASS THROUGH.
IF ALL GOES WELL, WE CAN JUST WAIT THIS OUT.

I WISH IT WERE UNDER BETTER CIRCUMSTANCES, BUT IT'S REALLY NICE TO SEE YOU.
I'M SCARED OF WHAT QUALIFIES AS "BETTER CIRCUMSTANCES" FOR US.

BWAAAHMMMM!

BWAAAHMMM!
BWAAHMMM!

THAT GOT THEIR ATTENTION.

YOU KNOW THE PLAN, EVERYONE!
PULL THEM OUT OF THE CITY! DRIVE THEM WEST! ONCE THEY'RE ON THEIR WAY, CIRCLE BACK.
GO! GO! GO!

YOU SURE YOU DON'T NEED ME TO GO?
WITH A HERD THIS SIZE, THERE'S NO WAY THEY CAN DRAW THEM ALL OUT OF TOWN. I'LL NEED YOUR HELP ORGANIZING THE TOWNSPEOPLE SO THEY CAN CLEAR OUT THE STRAGGLERS.

SURE, SURE.
YOU JUST WANT TO KEEP ME CLOSE.

THE THOUGHT HAD CROSSED MY MIND.

WHATEVER THEY'RE DOING IS WORKING. THE DEAD ARE STARTING TO HEAD THE OTHER WAY.
GET AWAY FROM THE DAMN WINDOW!
IF THEY SEE YOU, WHAT THEY'RE DOING IS GOING TO STOP WORKING.

I DON'T KNOW WHY THEY'RE HERE, BUT THOSE ARE MY PEOPLE. THAT WAS THE HORN WE USE TO STEER THE HERDS IN OUR AREA. THEY KNOW WHAT THEY'RE DOING. THEY'LL CLEAR THE TOWN.
ALL WE NEED TO DO NOW IS STAY QUIET AND WAIT.

WE CLEAR THE DEAD OUT OF THE CITY AND THEN WHAT?

WE'LL SEND FOR GOVERNOR MILTON TO COME BACK, AND THEN WE'LL TALK.

AND WHAT IF SHE DOESN'T WANT TO TALK?

WE WON'T GIVE HER A CHOICE.

SHEEEH

LOOKS LIKE IT'S ABOUT THAT TIME.
IT'S THINNED OUT QUITE A BIT AND THEY'RE NOT REALLY MOVING, SO WHAT'S LEFT HAS CLEARLY BROKEN AWAY FROM THE HERD.

ALRIGHT, MEN! SUIT UP!

LET THEM TAKE THE LEAD. THEIR ARMOR IS QUITE EFFECTIVE.

SHUKK!
SHAKK!
WROKK!

SVAASH!

SHUKK!

SVAASH!

KEEP MOVING AND DON'T LET YOURSELF GET SURROUNDED!
LIKE I SHOWED YOU--STAB AND MOVE!

SHUKK!
OH, GOD!
OH, GOD!

IF YOU CAN'T HANDLE IT, GO BACK INSIDE UNTIL IT'S OVER!
THOK!

WELCOME TO THE COMMONWEALTH.

IT'S... UH, LOOKED BETTER.

WHAT BROUGHT THIS ON, MAGGIE? I KNOW YOU SENT CARL AND THE REST TO CHECK ON US, BUT THEN YOU IMMEDIATELY BROUGHT ALL THESE PEOPLE?
I DON'T KNOW. I JUST HAD A BAD FEELING, I GUESS.

YOU BROUGHT ALL THESE PEOPLE HERE ON A HUNCH?

YEAH, I GUESS I DID.

WELL, THANKS.

IT LOOKS LIKE YOU DIDN'T NEED US.
YOU HAD MORE THAN ENOUGH HELP ON THE WAY.

OH, SHIT.

YOU THINK I CAN'T SEE WHAT IS HAPPENING HERE?!
YOU THINK YOUR GOVERNOR IS *BLIND* TO THE PLOTS YOU'VE BEEN HATCHING *BEHIND MY BACK?!*

WHAT?!
WHAT ARE YOU TALKING ABOUT?!

YOU LIED TO ME, RICK GRIMES. YOU PRETENDED TO HELP ME--TO GET ME OUT OF HARM'S WAY!
YOU WERE REALLY GETTING ME OUT OF HERE SO YOU COULD BRING YOUR ARMY INTO THE COMMONWEALTH.
YOU WERE CONSPIRING WITH MERCER THE WHOLE TIME!

THAT IS NOT REMOTELY TRUE!
I HAVE ONLY EVER BEEN WORKING TO KEEP THE PEACE HERE-- TO HOLD THE COMMONWEALTH TOGETHER.
LIES!
I'M NOT FALLING FOR YOUR BULLSHIT ANYMORE!

PLEASE... CALM DOWN. WE CAN TALK THIS OVER.

YOU STAND WITH YOUR ARMY AND CLAIM YOU WANT TO TALK?! THE ARMY OF GREENVILLE STANDS WITH ME--AND WE WON'T STAND FOR YOUR DECEPTION.
FOR THE PEOPLE OF THE COMMONWEALTH-- FOR OUR FUTURE--

ATTACK!!

NO!
STOP!

PLEASE.
WE DON'T HAVE TO DO THIS. WE HAVE TIME... WE CAN TALK.
WE CAN WORK THIS OUT.
PLEASE.

WHAT ARE YOU DOING?!

THEY'RE BEING REASONABLE, PAMELA.
SOMETHING I KNOW YOU'RE CAPABLE OF. I'VE SEEN IT.
TRY IT AGAIN... UNLESS YOU WANT TO FIGHT THIS FIGHT ON YOUR OWN?

THAT'S WHAT I THOUGHT.

WE DON'T WANT TO FIGHT. I CAN SEE THAT.
KILLING EACH OTHER WILL ONLY SUCCEED IN COSTING SOME OF US OUR LIVES. I THINK WE'VE ALL BEEN THROUGH SO MUCH--TOO MUCH.
LET'S NOT DO THAT AGAIN.

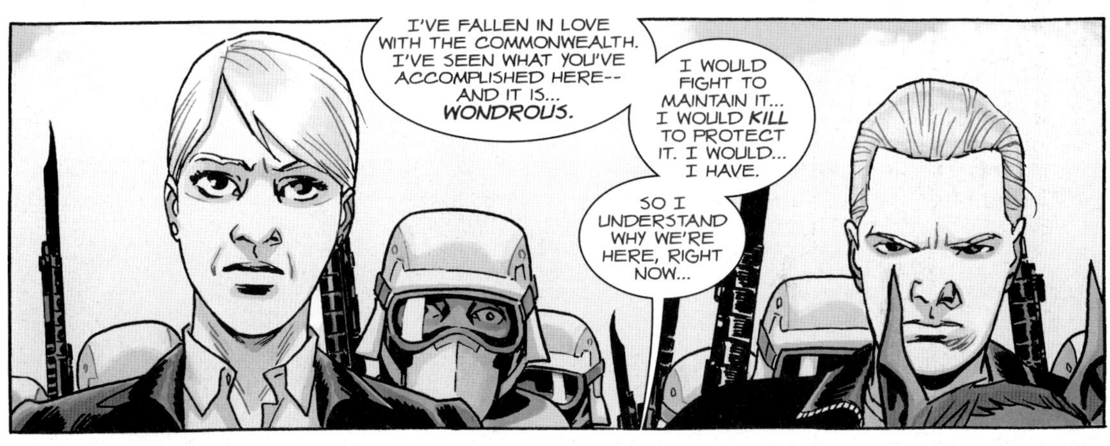
I'VE FALLEN IN LOVE WITH THE COMMONWEALTH. I'VE SEEN WHAT YOU'VE ACCOMPLISHED HERE--AND IT IS... WONDROUS.
I WOULD FIGHT TO MAINTAIN IT... I WOULD KILL TO PROTECT IT. I WOULD... I HAVE.
SO I UNDERSTAND WHY WE'RE HERE, RIGHT NOW...

BUT I LOOK AROUND, AND I SEE FEAR AND ANGER... AND HATRED.
THAT'S NOT WHAT THIS PLACE IS ABOUT.
THAT'S NOT WHO WE ARE.

THIS IS WHO WE ARE!

THIS WORLD HAS SCARRED US, MENTALLY AND PHYSICALLY.
WE CARRY THOSE SCARS WITH US-- EACH AND EVERY DAY.

THEY SERVE AS A REMINDER OF WHAT WE'VE LIVED THROUGH-- WHAT WE'VE DONE TO SURVIVE--WHAT OTHERS HAVE DONE TO US TO SURVIVE...
SACRIFICES MADE... ALL TO GET US HERE.
TO THIS POINT.

TO HAVE SO MANY OF US HERE. TO BE SAFE. TO BE CLOSE TO THE WAY THINGS WERE BEFORE.

I USED TO THINK WE HAD TO PUT OUR HUMANITY ON HOLD... EMBRACE A... SAVAGENESS IN ORDER TO SURVIVE... BECAUSE OUR WORLD, THE ONE WE KNEW, WAS NEVER COMING BACK.

I WAS WRONG.

WE ARE ON THE ROAD BACK, I CAN SEE OUR FUTURE AHEAD OF US, AND IT IS BRIGHT.
WE NO LONGER LIVE SURROUNDED BY THE DEAD. WE'RE NOT AMONG THEM--NOT LIVING ON BORROWED TIME...

WE DO NOT LIVE MINUTE TO MINUTE, IN MINUTES STOLEN FROM THE DEAD. WE CAN BE HAPPY... WE CAN BE CONTENT... WE CAN HAVE PEACE.
WE CAN LIVE AGAIN.

WE ARE NOT THE WALKING DEAD!

AT LEAST... WE DON'T *HAVE* TO BE.
NOT ANYMORE.

I THINK OF THIS WORLD AS A GIFT... EVEN AFTER ALL THE PAIN IT'S CAUSED ME. IT'S A CHANCE TO REBUILD THINGS... BETTER THAN THEY WERE BEFORE.
WE HAVEN'T WORKED AS HARD AS WE HAVE JUST TO BRING BACK OLD, FLAWED, UNFAIR SYSTEMS.
WE DESERVE A *BETTER* WORLD.

A WORLD WE WILL *APPRECIATE*... BECAUSE OF WHAT WE'VE JUST LIVED THROUGH.
WE SHOULD HAVE AN ELEVATED SENSE OF *RESPECT* FOR EACH OTHER... BECAUSE WE KNOW WHAT WE'VE *ALL* LIVED THROUGH.

BUT THAT'S NOT THE CASE, IS IT?
WE DON'T SEEM TO HAVE THAT RESPECT FOR EACH OTHER.
AND YOU'RE CLINGING TO OLD WAYS... WHERE THE FEW LIVE IN A POSITION *OVER* THE MANY.
...

WHY?

GOVERNOR MILTON... I SEE NOW I WAS WRONG TO SUPPORT YOU. I WAS TRYING TO KEEP THE PEACE, HOPING YOU WOULD SEE THE ERROR OF YOUR WAYS EVENTUALLY... THAT CHANGE COULD COME FROM WITHIN.
NOW I SEE YOU FOR WHAT YOU TRULY ARE... SOMEONE WHO CRAVES POWER ABOVE ALL ELSE.

YOU WOULD LEAD YOUR PEOPLE... INTO KILLING EACH OTHER...
JUST TO MAINTAIN THAT *POWER?*

I ASK YOU, PEOPLE OF THE COMMONWEALTH... IS THAT THE KIND OF LEADER YOU WANT?
THAT YOU *DESERVE?*

NO!

THEN LET YOUR VOICE BE HEARD!
TAKE CHARGE OF YOUR LIVES... BRING ABOUT A COMMONWEALTH THAT WORKS FOR YOU... RATHER THAN AGAINST YOU.
IF YOU DON'T WANT PAMELA MILTON TO LEAD YOU--THEN DON'T LET HER LEAD YOU!

I'M SORRY, MA'AM. I THINK THIS IS FOR THE BEST--FOR YOUR OWN SAFETY.
JUST FUCKING GET IT OVER WITH.

...

SHOW'S OVER HERE--
LET'S ALL GO HOME.

WHAT?!
YOU THINK YOU CAN JUST ARREST MY MOM?!
WE FUCKING BUILT THIS PLACE! YOU THINK YOU CAN KEEP IT RUNNING WITHOUT US?!
YOU NEED US! YOU'RE FUCKING LOST WITHOUT US!

SEBASTIAN!

...

UNLESS YOU WANT TO END UP IN A CELL RIGHT NEXT TO ME--
SHUT THE FUCK UP!

WE MIGHT ACTUALLY FINISH BEFORE SUNDOWN.

AMAZING WHAT WE CAN ACCOMPLISH WHEN WE ALL WORK TOGETHER, ISN'T IT?

THIS IS CRAZY. THERE ARE PEOPLE OUT HERE WORKING WHO I'VE NEVER SEEN LIFT A FINGER IN THIS TOWN BEFORE.
YOU'VE INSPIRED THEM.

OR SCARED THEM.
WHATEVER WORKS.

CARE TO GIVE US A HAND?

WHAT AN ASSHOLE.

COME TO GLOAT?
NOT EVEN A LITTLE BIT.

I CAME TO *APOLOGIZE.* THINGS GOT A LITTLE OUT OF HAND OUT THERE.
I JUST WANTED TO PREVENT BLOODSHED... I DIDN'T INTEND FOR IT TO END IN YOUR ARREST, BUT WHEN MERCER STARTED TO TAKE YOU AWAY, I REALIZED THAT MAYBE PEOPLE WERE TOO WORKED UP.
YOU WERE SAFER HERE.

I FORGET... WHO WAS IT THAT WORKED THEM UP IN THE FIRST PLACE?

YOUR POWER WAS THREATENED, AND YOU LED AN ARMY BACK HERE TO SLAUGHTER YOUR OWN PEOPLE.
YOU'RE REALLY GOING TO CRITICIZE WHAT I DID?

SLAUGHTER IS A STRONG WORD... I DIDN'T... I GOT CARRIED AWAY.
I FEEL LIKE FOR THE COMMONWEALTH TO SUCCEED... I NEED TO BE IN CONTROL. YOU DON'T KNOW HOW COMPLICATED THINGS ARE HERE.
I THOUGHT I WAS *SAVING* LIVES BY STAYING IN CHARGE.

I THINK YOU ACTUALLY BELIEVE THAT... DESPITE IT BEING COMPLETELY WRONG.
I KNOW HOW MUCH PRESSURE YOU'RE UNDER EVERY DAY... I'VE MADE MY SHARE OF MISTAKES MYSELF.

SO THAT'S WHAT THIS WAS TO YOU?
A MISTAKE?

I'M IN A GENEROUS MOOD.
KLINK.

YOU'RE LETTING ME GO?

THERE'S A GAPING HOLE IN THE WALL A FEW CELLS DOWN. I DON'T KNOW HOW SAFE THIS BUILDING IS.
AND I FIGURED YOU'D PREFER TO SLEEP IN YOUR OWN BED TONIGHT.

DO I STILL HAVE MY OWN BED? OR ARE YOU GOING TO ESCORT ME TO SOME COMMUNAL TENT?
I'M NOT KICKING YOU OUT OF YOUR HOME.

HOW DOES THAT WORK? SOME OF US HAVE MUCH NICER HOMES THAN OTHERS... NOT EXACTLY FAIR, IS IT?
WHO EARNS THE NICER HOMES? WHO DECIDES NOW?

I DON'T KNOW.
WE'LL JUST HAVE TO FIGURE THAT OUT... TOGETHER.

YOU'RE NAÏVE.
AND YOU'VE GOT A COUPLE GUARDS WAITING TO ESCORT YOU HOME.
GO.

YOU SURE ABOUT THIS?
SHE POSES NO THREAT-- NO ONE WANTS HER IN CHARGE ANYMORE.
YOU THINK SHE'LL BE SAFE?

EVERYONE IS SO HAPPY AND OPTIMISTIC... I THINK SHE'LL BE FINE.
I'LL KEEP GUARDS ON WATCH NEAR HER PLACE JUST IN CASE.

I'M TOLD MORALE INSIDE THE COMMONWEALTH IS AT AN ALL-TIME HIGH.
EVERYONE IS HAPPY AND OPTIMISTIC FOR THE FUTURE. CANDIDATES ARE LINING UP FOR THE FIRST ORGANIZED ELECTION HERE.
ALTHOUGH... THERE'S A CLEAR FRONT RUNNER.

ME?

YEAH, WHO DO YOU THINK?
YOU'VE ***INSPIRED*** THESE PEOPLE... THE SAME WAY YOU ALWAYS DO. YOU'RE A FUCKING ROCK STAR, RICK GRIMES.

YOU LAID THE GROUNDWORK. YOU MADE QUITE A SPLASH HERE BEFORE I EVEN GOT HERE.
DON'T LAY THIS ALL ON MY FEET. BESIDES, I WON'T BE RUNNING. MY PLACE IS IN ALEXANDRIA. WE HAVE OUR OWN PROBLEMS.

REALLY? AS I RECALL, YOU'VE FIXED ALL OF THOSE, TOO.

YOU'VE ALWAYS GIVEN US THINGS TO LIVE FOR.
PEOPLE NEED THAT. WE'LL ***ALWAYS*** NEED THAT.
WE'LL ALWAYS NEED YOU.

SO ARE YOU GOING TO DO IT?
RUN FOR GOVERNOR?
NO.
DEFINITELY NOT.

YOU COULD CALL IT SOMETHING DIFFERENT.
THAT'S NOT IT.

IF I COME IN, TAKE OVER... PAMELA'S RIGHT. PEOPLE WILL START TO REALIZE THAT. THEY'LL TURN... TRUST ME.
THE COMMONWEALTH NEEDS TO GROW FROM WITHIN. IT NEEDS TO BE SOMEONE WHO ALREADY LIVES HERE.

HOW DO YOU DO THAT?
DO WHAT?

I DON'T KNOW, DAD... FROM MY PERSPECTIVE, IT SEEMS LIKE YOU CAN SEE THE FUTURE.
HOW DO YOU ALWAYS KNOW WHAT'S RIGHT?

SAME WAY YOU ALWAYS DO.
IT'S JUST A FEELING.

MY FEELING IS SOMETIMES WRONG.

MINE IS, TOO... ALL THE TIME.
YOU JUST HAVE TO REALIZE, THIS WORLD NEEDS PEOPLE WHO ARE WILLING TO STAND UP AND DO THE RIGHT THING... IT NEEDS THEM SO BADLY, IT'LL FORGIVE YOU IF YOU'RE SOMETIMES WRONG.
YOU NEED TO JUST MAKE SURE THE LOSSES DON'T DISCOURAGE YOU... BECAUSE THE PEOPLE AROUND US... THEY'LL ALWAYS NEED THE WINS.

...

I'M PROUD YOU'RE MY FATHER.

CARL...
I'M PROUD YOU'RE MY SON.

I'M, UH... THEY WERE ABLE TO GET ME A ROOM HERE.
SO... THIS IS MY STOP.
OH, I DIDN'T EVEN KNOW THIS WAS A HOTEL. OKAY, THEN.
GOOD NIGHT.

GOOD NIGHT, DAD.

WHAT--?

DON'T MAKE A FUCKING SOUND.
DON'T MOVE.

SEBASTIAN, TRUST ME--
YOU DON'T WANT TO DO THIS.

WHAT I DON'T WANT TO DO IS WATCH ALL MY HARD WORK--MY MOTHER'S HARD WORK--GO DOWN THE FUCKING DRAIN BECAUSE OF YOU.
I DON'T WANT TO SEE THE COMMONWEALTH FALL APART!
YOU'VE DISRUPTED THE NATURAL ORDER OF THINGS--YOU'VE RUINED EVERYTHING!

PUT THE GUN DOWN.

UNLIKE EVERYONE ELSE--YOU CAN'T TELL ME WHAT TO DO!

I'VE HEARD YOUR PEOPLE--HOW THEY TALK ABOUT YOU. I HEARD ABOUT YOU LONG BEFORE YOU GOT HERE. THEY THINK YOU'RE A SAVIOR--ALMOST LIKE YOU'RE SOME KIND OF GOD.
PEOPLE ARE STARTING TO TALK ABOUT YOU LIKE THAT HERE, TOO. ONE SPEECH AND MY FAMILY IS KICKED OUT. I'M SUPPOSED TO JUST PRETEND I'M LIKE EVERYONE ELSE NOW? BECAUSE YOU SAID SO?
YOU'RE THAT POWERFUL, HUH?
YOU FEEL POWERFUL NOW?

WELL?!
DO YOU?!
DON'T.

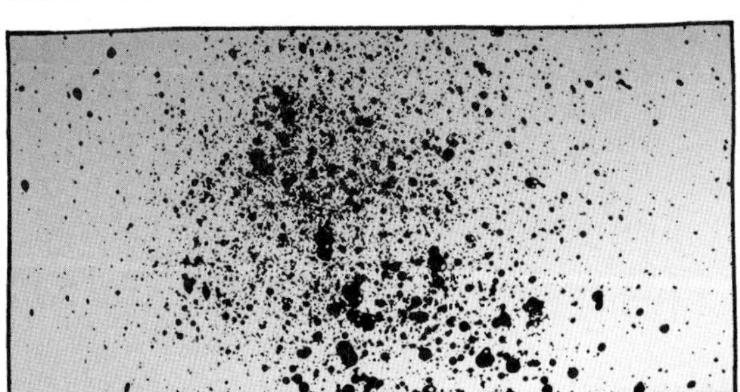

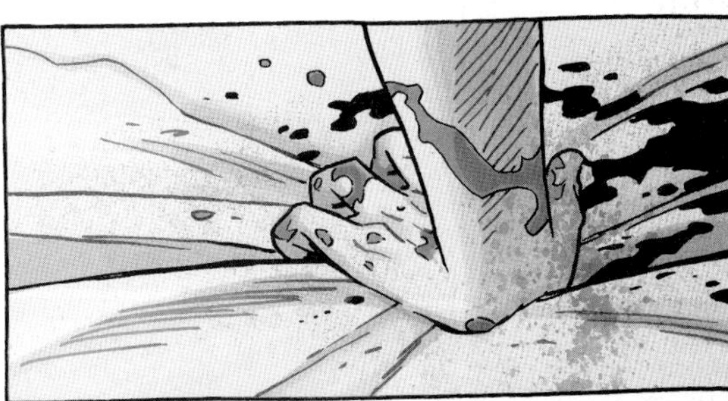

I--
I--

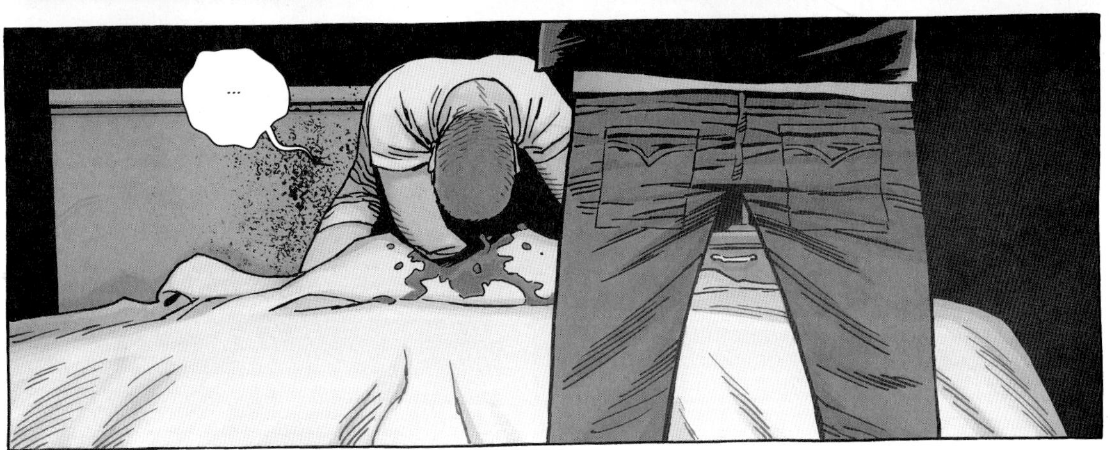
...

WHAT DID YOU DO?

WHAT--?

I'M SORRY.
I DIDN'T...

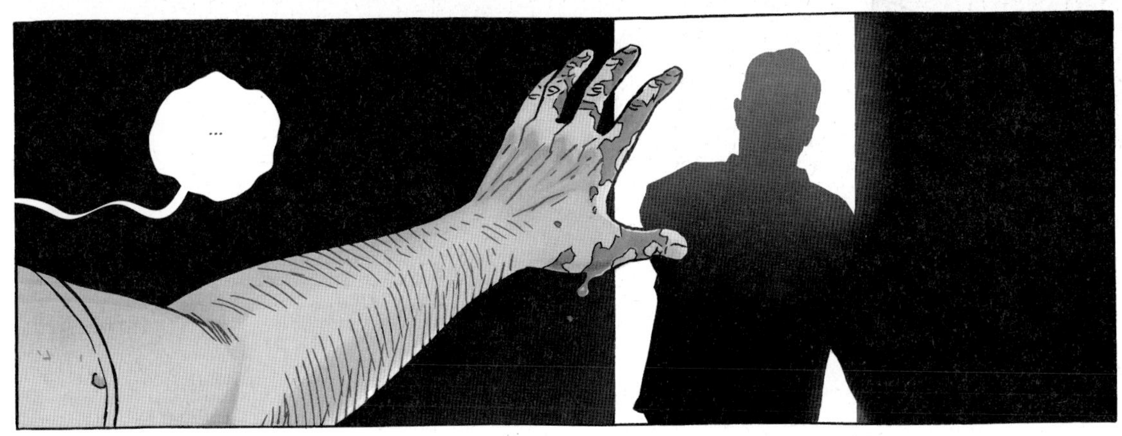
...

SPAK!

SPAK!SPAK!

WHUMP.

KLAKK!

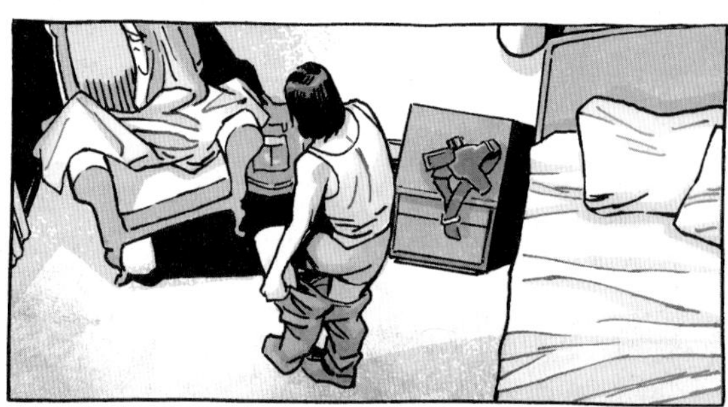

SLEEP WELL?
SURE DID.

MAN... THIS PLACE REALLY CLEANS UP NICE.
WOW.
THERE'S A RESTAURANT UP THE STREET THAT SERVES THE BEST PANCAKES. YOU SHOULD GIVE IT A SHOT.
YOU HAD ME AT PANCAKES. LET ME SEE IF MY DAD'S UP.

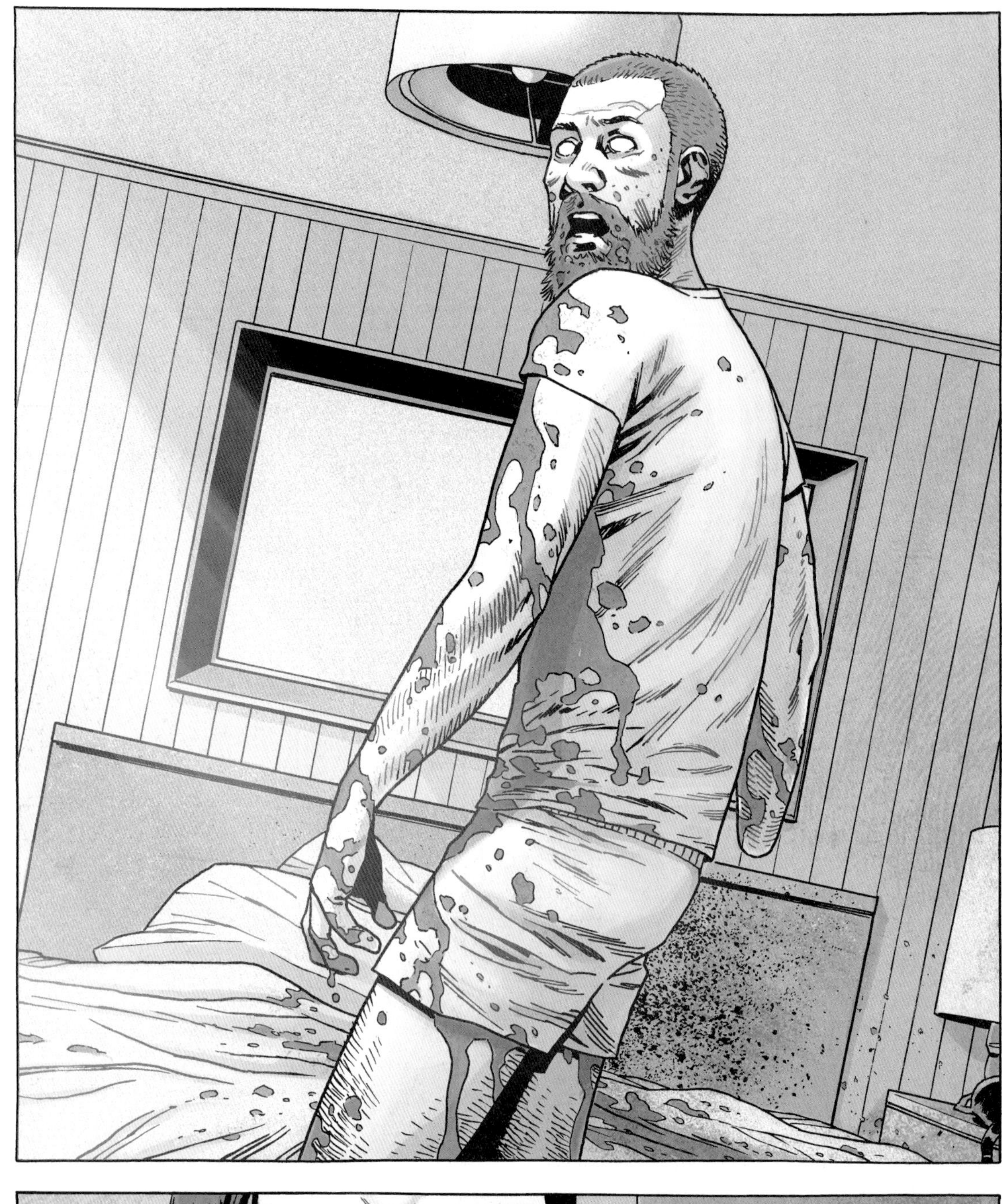

BLAM!

WHUMP.

LOOK, THE DOOR IS OPEN!
DON'T GO IN! SEND FOR A GUARD!

OH, GOD--!
GO GET MERCER! FIND HIM!

JESUS...
I THINK I KNOW WHOSE GUN THIS IS.

HIS SON. YES.
SEND FOR MICHONNE... SHE'LL KNOW WHAT TO DO.

I DIDN'T EVEN SEE HIM.
I JUST SAW THE DEAD... I REACTED. BY THE TIME HE WAS ON THE GROUND... I REALIZED WHAT I'D DONE.

WHEN I WAS A KID, WHEN WE WERE ALONE IN THAT HOUSE AFTER WE'D ESCAPED THE PRISON... I REMEMBER I THOUGHT HE WAS DEAD.
I WAS SO SCARED OF BEING ALONE... I HESITATED. LIKE I THOUGHT DYING WOULD BE BETTER THAN LIVING WITHOUT HIM.

TODAY WAS DIFFERENT, BUT...

I'M STILL SCARED OF LIVING WITHOUT HIM.

OH, CARL.

I KEEP THINKING... WHAT IF I'D JUST GONE TO BREAKFAST WITHOUT HIM? IF I HADN'T GONE TO HIS ROOM...
HE WAS TIRED, I SHOULD HAVE JUST... LET HIM SLEEP.

HE'D HAVE BEEN *ALIVE* A LITTLE LONGER.
I MEAN... NOT REALLY. BUT KIND OF.
I WISH I DIDN'T KNOW.

IF I'D STAYED AT THE HILLTOP... I WOULDN'T *KNOW.*

WHAT DO YOU WANT?

IT TOOK TWO DAYS... BUT WE FOUND YOUR FATHER'S KILLER.
IT'S MY SON, SEBASTIAN.

WHERE IS HE?

HE'S IN CUSTODY.
I WANT TO TALK TO YOU DIRECTLY. MAKE YOU AWARE OF THE SITUATION... GET YOUR... TAKE ON THINGS.

WHAT DO YOU MEAN?

THIS IS A VERY EMOTIONAL TIME FOR YOU. YOU'VE BEEN THROUGH... SO MUCH... AND...
I'M SO VERY SORRY.
I JUST... WANT TO MAKE SURE YOU'RE NOT GOING TO... TAKE MATTERS INTO YOUR OWN HANDS.

WILL HE BE PUNISHED?

HE'S MY SON, I LOVE HIM WITH ALL MY HEART...
BUT HE'LL SPEND THE REST OF HIS LIFE BEHIND BARS FOR WHAT HE DID.

OKAY THEN.

I'M SORRY FOR WHAT YOU'RE GOING THROUGH.

I'M SORRY FOR WHAT SEBASTIAN DID, TOO. I KNOW THIS IS A HARD TIME FOR YOU.
BUT IF YOU THINK SOMEHOW YOU'RE JUST GOING TO QUIETLY TAKE THAT DESK BACK BECAUSE OF ALL THIS...
DON'T.

YOU'RE HIS SON... AREN'T YOU?

I DON'T KNOW WHAT TO SAY TO YOU.

MY MOTHER RAN THIS PLACE. MY DAD DIED A LONG TIME AGO. MY SISTER, TOO. EVERYTHING WAS BAD... UNTIL WE GOT *HERE.*
ONCE THE COMMONWEALTH WAS UP AND RUNNING... LIFE HAD NEVER BEEN BETTER. WE MADE THE RULES, WE WERE ON TOP. I DID WHATEVER I WANTED.
I THOUGHT I COULD DO *ANYTHING.*
SO WHEN YOUR DAD FUCKED EVERYTHING UP... I THOUGHT... IF HE WENT AWAY, EVERYTHING WOULD GO BACK TO NORMAL.

I'VE... NEVER KILLED ANYONE BEFORE.
I KNOW SO MANY PEOPLE HAVE... SO MANY DANGEROUS PEOPLE OUT THERE... BUT I HAVEN'T.

THEY ALWAYS SAY... TAKING A LIFE IS HARD.

BUT IT WASN'T... IT WAS...
IT WAS *SO EASY.*

SHUT UP.

YOU THINK I'M GOING TO FEEL SORRY FOR YOU NOW?
EVERYONE HAS BEEN TALKING ABOUT YOU. NO ONE LIKES YOU. NO ONE EVER LIKED YOU.
YOU'RE NOT A GOOD PERSON. I CAN TELL. YOU'RE NOT SAD ABOUT WHAT YOU DID... YOU'RE SAD ABOUT WHAT HAPPENED TO YOU BECAUSE OF IT.

YOUR MOTHER WAS WORRIED I WAS GOING TO TAKE MATTERS IN MY OWN HANDS. KILL YOU... FOR REVENGE.
I LIKE THIS BETTER.
I GET TO CHECK ON YOU. SEE YOUR MISERY. YOU GET TO SIT AND REMEMBER THE LIFE YOU HAD. THAT'S A FAR BETTER PUNISHMENT THAN DEATH.

MY DAD TAUGHT ME THAT.
IT'S MORE... CIVILIZED.

IT'S WHAT HE WOULD HAVE WANTED.

ALL THAT ASIDE... MAKE NO MISTAKE...
IF YOU *EVER* GET OUT OF THIS CELL FOR *ANY* REASON...

I WILL FIND YOU... AND BEFORE I PUT YOU BACK IN THIS CELL...
I WILL HURT YOU.

...

I'LL BE SEEING YOU.
TA-TA.

ALL SET?

YEAH.
I KNOW THERE ARE PEOPLE WHO WANTED TO BURY HIM HERE, BUT... HE SHOULD BE BURIED NEXT TO ANDREA. IT'S WHAT HE WOULD HAVE WANTED.
I COMPLETELY AGREE.

YOU DON'T HAVE TO COME WITH ME.
I CAN MAKE IT ON MY OWN.

I'M SURE YOU CAN. BUT YOU SHOULDN'T.
I'M SURE YOU COULD USE THE COMPANY.

CARL, I KNOW YOU WANTED TO GET AN EARLY START... BUT THERE'S SOME PEOPLE WHO WANT TO PAY THEIR RESPECTS IN ALEXANDRIA.
SHOULDN'T TAKE MORE THAN AN HOUR OR SO FOR THEM TO PACK UP.

WAIT... WHO WANTS TO COME?

CARL?!

CARL!

ARE YOU OKAY?

HE SACRIFICED SO MUCH TO CREATE A WORLD WHERE WE CAN SAY GOODBYE... ANDREA... SHE GOT TO SAY GOODBYE TO EVERYONE.
BUT HE...
HE'S JUST... GONE.

WHAT WAS IT ALL FOR?

EVERYTHING IS BETTER NOW... SAFER... THE WHOLE WORLD... IS DIFFERENT.
BECAUSE OF HIM.

HE SURVIVED... SO MUCH.
BUT NOW?
NOW HE DIES?!
OH, GOD...

I CAN'T GO ON WITHOUT HIM.

I CAN'T *DO* THIS...
NOT ANYMORE.

THUMP!
THUMP!
THUMP!

HURNN?

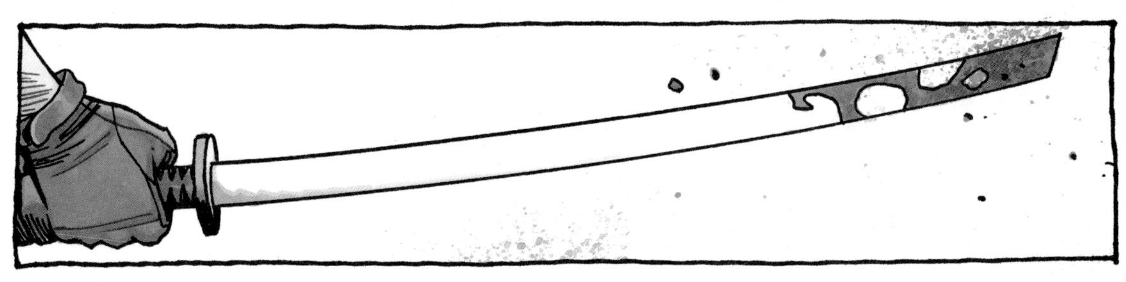

CARL?!
CARL!

I ALREADY KILLED IT, SOPHIA.
IT'S DEAD.

I DON'T GET WHY YOU COULDN'T HAVE USED A GUN.
I DON'T LIKE YOU BEING SO CLOSE TO ONE... AFTER ALL THESE YEARS.

WHAT IF THERE WERE MORE WE DIDN'T SEE?

HERE? THAT'S NOT POSSIBLE.
NOT ANYMORE.

WAIT!
WHERE'S ANDREA?! DID SHE SEE IT?

SHE'S NOT EVEN UP YET. DON'T WORRY.
YOU KNOW SHE DOESN'T WAKE UP ON A SCHOOL DAY UNLESS I DRAG HER OUT OF BED.

WHAT ARE YOU DOING?
MAKING SURE IT DIDN'T BITE ANYONE.
IT LOOKS CLEAN.

I JUST DON'T UNDERSTAND. HOW COULD A ROAMER GET HERE? THERE ARE SO MANY CHECKPOINTS, SO MANY BARRIERS TO GET PAST... TO GET THIS FAR INSIDE THE SAFE ZONE...
IT JUST DOESN'T MAKE SENSE.

IT'S JUST ONE. MAYBE IT SOMEHOW SLIPPED THROUGH?

NO. THAT CAN'T--
WAIT!
IS HERSHEL IN TOWN?!

SEE THE WALKING DEAD
DON'T GET TOO CLOSE!

HOLY SHIT-- CARL GRIMES?!
IS THAT YOU?!

LOOK AT YOU, YOU LIVING LEGEND! IT'S GREAT TO SEE YOU, MAN.
YOU WANT TO SEE THE SHOW? I'D BE HAPPY TO HOOK YOU UP.

WRAMM!

WHUDD!

WHAT--?!

HOW MANY ARE IN THE CART, HERSHEL?!
HOW MANY?!

DID YOU FIND IT?!
OH MY GOD-- I'M SO GLAD IT WAS YOU, CARL! I WAS SO WORRIED IT WOULD HURT SOMEONE!
WHERE IS IT?!

IT'S GONE.
I KILLED IT.

WHAT?!

YOU KILLED IT?! IT'S FUCKING DEAD?!
ARE YOU KIDDING?! TELL ME YOU'RE KIDDING!
DO YOU HAVE ANY IDEA HOW MUCH THESE THINGS ARE WORTH?!
DON'T GET TOO CLOSE

WHERE ARE YOU--

COME BACK HERE! I'M GETTING SHERIFF KAPOOR!
THIS IS OUTRAGEOUS!

THE SHERIFF KNOWS WHERE I LIVE...

SCHOOL IS FUN SOMETIMES, BUT NOT EVERY DAY. TODAY WE LEARNED MUSIC STUFF. I LIKE THAT.
MUSIC IS FUN.
THAT'S AWESOME. I CAN'T WAIT TO GET HOME AND FIND OUT IF ADITYA ENJOYED TODAY'S CLASS AS MUCH AS YOU DID, ANDREA.
I'LL BE SURE TO TELL HIM I SAW YOU, BUT RIGHT NOW, I KIND OF NEED TO TALK TO YOUR DADDY.

ANDREA--GO TO YOUR ROOM AND PICK OUT A DRESS FOR TONIGHT. WE'RE HAVING DINNER OVER AT THE SUTTON FARM.
OKAY!
SORRY, SHE GETS EXCITED WHENEVER WE HAVE COMPANY.
IT'S OKAY. SHE'S ADORABLE.

I'M REALLY SORRY HERSHEL BOTHERED YOU WITH THIS SHIT, BUT IT'S GOOD YOU'RE HERE. YOU CAN HELP ME GET RID OF THAT THING. YOU KNOW A GOOD PLACE TO BURN IT? I FIGURED THAT'D BE BEST.
I'M SORRY, CARL... BUT THINGS AREN'T QUITE THAT SIMPLE. YOU'RE TALKING ABOUT BURNING EVIDENCE. THIS IS DESTRUCTION OF PRIVATE PROPERTY... THE LAW IS VERY CLEAR.

THE LAW--?!

THAT THING COULD HAVE KILLED SOMEBODY!

BUT IT DIDN'T.
AS IT STANDS RIGHT NOW... IT WAS PERSONAL PROPERTY AND YOU DESTROYED IT. I'M NOT CRAZY. I KNOW THE DANGERS OF WHAT COULD HAVE HAPPENED...
BUT THE LAW IS ONLY CONCERNED WITH WHAT DID.

YOU CAN'T BE SERIOUS.

I'M SORRY, BUT I AM.
I KNOW WE GO WAY BACK, THAT'S WHY YOU'RE NOT UNDER ARREST, AND I'M GOING TO DO EVERYTHING IN MY POWER TO HELP YOU.
WE'RE GOING TO HAVE AN INFORMAL HEARING ABOUT THE INCIDENT TOMORROW. HOPEFULLY WE CAN KEEP YOUR PUNISHMENT DOWN TO A FINE OR SOMETHING.
A FINE?!

I'M SORRY, CARL. THAT'S THE BEST I CAN DO.
I'LL... SEE YOU TOMORROW.

I TOLD YOU THAT JOB WAS DANGEROUS, BOY! YOU SHOULD HAVE STAYED A SMITH, LIKE MIKEY.

NO, EARL. I TOLD YOU, IT DIDN'T HAPPEN ON A RUN. IT WAS AT MY HOUSE. THAT'S WHY I'M SO MAD AT HERSHEL.
HE BROUGHT THOSE THINGS TO TOWN, AND THEN LET ONE GO. HE PUT US ALL IN DANGER.
IT'S OVER NOW, THOUGH. NOTHING TO WORRY ABOUT. IT'S ALL BEEN TAKEN CARE OF... BUT THAT'S THE THING. IT SEEMS THEY'RE GOING TO TRY TO PUNISH CARL FOR WHAT HE DID.

THAT'S IMPOSSIBLE. THERE HASN'T BEEN A ROAMER IN THESE PARTS FOR DAMN NEAR TEN YEARS.
HOW WOULD IT HAVE GOTTEN PAST THE PATROLS?

...

I WAS JUST TENDING TO MY ROSE BUSHES TODAY. ALL CLEAR. ANOTHER GLORIOUS DAY.
THANKS TO THAT FAMOUS FATHER OF YOURS.

YOU KNOW, MAYBE YOU SHOULD CONSIDER MOVING INTO TOWN.
THERE'S A LOVELY COMMUNITY FOR PEOPLE YOUR AGE. BRIANNA IS SO HAPPY THERE.
WE'D SURE WORRY ABOUT YOU A LOT LESS.

NO.
I SHOULD HAVE LEFT THE HILLTOP AFTER THE THIRD EXPANSION. I'VE DONE MY TIME IN CIVILIZATION.
I LIKE LIVING OUT HERE, HOW QUIET IT IS. ALSO... I CAN'T LEAVE YOU GUYS ON YOUR OWN. WHAT WOULD YOU DO WITHOUT YOUR CRANKY OLD NEIGHBOR?

ARE YOU SURE YOU WANT US TO TAKE ALL THIS FOOD WITH US?
IT'LL JUST SPOIL BEFORE I GET AROUND TO IT.
WELL, THANK YOU, EARL.
THANKS FOR HAVING US.

THAT BOY WASN'T RAISED RIGHT. MAGGIE WAS SO BUSY WITH EVERYTHING AT THE COMMONWEALTH AFTER YOUR DAD DIED THAT SHE JUST... GAVE HIM EVERYTHING HE WANTED.
AND THAT'S ONLY WHEN SHE WAS AROUND... WHICH WASN'T OFTEN.
HERSHEL'S ALWAYS BEEN TROUBLE.

UH... YEAH.
YOU THINK I'M NOT PAYING ATTENTION SOMETIMES... BUT I AM.

SHARP AS EVER, EARL.
YOU HAVE A GOOD NIGHT.

NIGHT WAS ALWAYS SO SCARY... I NEVER APPRECIATED THE STARS.
I REMEMBER.

SOMETHING SO BEAUTIFUL... AND STILL, IT FILLS ME WITH DREAD.
THINGS ARE DIFFERENT NOW.

ARE THEY? FOR HOW MUCH LONGER?

YOU OKAY?

JUST THINKING ABOUT MY DAD...

YOU AND EVERYONE ELSE ALIVE... AT ALL TIMES.
HEH. YEAH.

HE NEVER EVEN GOT TO MEET ANDREA. SOMETIMES I THINK ABOUT THAT... AND IT MAKES ME SAD.
MORE THAN THAT, IT'S EARL. IT'S SO HARD TO SEE HOW HE IS NOW, HOW BAD HE'S GOTTEN.
I COULDN'T BEAR TO SEE MY DAD LIKE THAT. SO THEN I THINK... MAYBE IT'S GOOD THAT HE'S GONE... THAT I'VE BEEN SPARED SEEING HIM DETERIORATE. THAT WAY HE LIVES ON AS THIS... ICON.
BUT THAT'S HORRIFIC, SO WHEN I START THINKING LIKE THAT... I FEEL EVEN WORSE.

I JUST MISS HIM SO MUCH.

YOU DIDN'T HAVE TO DO THIS.

ANDREA'S IN SCHOOL... AND I'M WAY AHEAD WITH MY WRITING.
LET ME BE HERE FOR YOU, CARL. YOU DON'T HAVE TO CARRY EVERYTHING ON YOUR OWN.

UH...

SORRY... WORD MUST HAVE GOTTEN OUT ABOUT CARL GRIMES COMING INTO TOWN FOR A HEARING.
MY MEN WILL ESCORT YOU IN.

IT'S A RATHER **FULL HOUSE** TODAY. SO I NEED EVERYONE TO GET SITUATED AND TAKE YOUR SEATS.
ANY DISRUPTIONS AND I **WILL** CLEAR MY COURT.

WE FIND OURSELVES HERE TODAY TO DISCUSS A SIMPLE DISPUTE. I WILL ALLOW BOTH PARTIES TO TELL THEIR SIDE OF THE STORY. I WILL THEN CONFER WITH COUNCIL AND MAKE MY DECISION.
IT IS MY GOAL TO ENSURE A PEACEFUL AND SWIFT RESOLUTION TO THIS DISPUTE. SO WITH THAT IN MIND, HERSHEL GREENE HAS BEEN CHOSEN TO GO FIRST. I ASK YOU TO BE **BRIEF.**
AS MANY OF YOU KNOW, I MAKE MY LIVING WITH A TRAVELING SHOW. I HAVE SOME OF THE ONLY KNOWN ROAMERS IN THE SAFE ZONE. PEOPLE PAY ME TO SEE THESE DANGEROUS CREATURES UP CLOSE.
IT IS AT GREAT EXPENSE THAT I HAVE ACQUIRED THESE SPECIMENS. I WAS FRANTIC WHEN ONE OF THEM ESCAPED. I SPENT THE WHOLE NIGHT SEARCHING FOR IT...
ONLY TO DISCOVER THE NEXT MORNING THAT **CARL GRIMES** HAD FOUND IT... AND **DESTROYED** IT IMMEDIATELY.
YOU ALL KNOW, CARL HAS A FAMOUS FATHER... BUT THAT SHOULDN'T MEAN HE CAN DO WHATEVER HE WANTS WITHOUT ANY FEAR OF CONSEQUENCE.

OKAY...
I'M NOT... I'M SORRY, I'M A LITTLE NERVOUS.
I'VE NEVER BEEN TO ONE OF THESE HEARINGS. THIS IS NEW TO ME.

I'M NOT HERE TO DENY WHAT I DID. I SAW THAT THING ON MY LAND, WHERE MY WIFE AND DAUGHTER LIVE... AND I KNOW HOW DANGEROUS THEY CAN BE.
IT NEVER OCCURRED TO ME, FOR EVEN ONE SECOND, TO CONSIDER DOING SOMETHING OTHER THAN WHAT I DID.
KILL IT.

THAT'S WHAT I'VE DONE EVERY TIME I'VE EVER ENCOUNTERED ONE OF THEM, AND TO BE CLEAR, I'VE ENCOUNTERED MANY.
YOU HAVE TO KILL THEM BEFORE THEY KILL YOU.
I KNOW THAT'S NOT REALLY THE TIME WE LIVE IN ANYMORE. I KNOW THERE'S SO MANY OF YOU WHO BARELY REMEMBER WHAT LIFE WAS LIKE.

TO YOU... THE DEAD ARE A NOVELTY. SOMETHING TO PAY MONEY TO SEE... FOR ENTERTAINMENT.
I'M AWARE OF HOW... POPULAR HERSHEL'S SHOW IS.
DOESN'T MEAN I AGREE WITH IT.

I DID WHAT I DID. I DON'T REGRET IT. I WOULD DO IT AGAIN.
IF WE NOW LIVE IN A WORLD WHERE PROTECTING THE LIVING IS CAUSE FOR *PUNISHMENT...*
PUNISH ME.

BUT FORGIVE ME IF I'M *CERTAIN* MOST OF YOU, LIKE ME, ARE THANKFUL MY FATHER DIDN'T LIVE TO SEE US COME TO *THIS.*

...

OKAY...

THAT WAS CERTAINLY *DRAMATIC...* I THINK I HAVE MORE THAN ENOUGH TO MAKE MY JUDGEMENT.
IF COUNCIL WILL PLEASE SEE ME IN MY CHAMBERS, I WOULD LIKE TO...

SORRY I'M LATE.
I COULDN'T MAKE THE TRAIN LAST NIGHT. I CAME AS FAST AS I COULD...

MADAM PRESIDENT...

MOM!

MAY I SPEAK TO YOU?
CERTAINLY, MA'AM.

THANK YOU, MADAM PRESIDENT.

THERE WILL BE NO FORMAL PUNISHMENT FOR THE CHARGES.

WHAT?!

BUT MISTER GRIMES WILL BE REQUIRED BY LAW TO FIND A SUITABLE REPLACEMENT FOR THE DESTROYED SPECIMEN.

WHAT?!

THOSE ARE MY ORDERS. I SUGGEST YOU CARRY THEM OUT IN A REASONABLE TIME OR I'LL SEE YOU BACK HERE.
I'M CALLING FOR A SMALL RECESS BEFORE WE MOVE ONTO THE NEXT HEARING.

I THOUGHT I WAS GETTING YOU OFF EASY. YOU RUN INTO THOSE THINGS ALL THE TIME... CAN'T BE HARD TO BRING ONE BACK WITH YOU.
SHE WAS GOING TO FINE YOU THE COST OF THE ROAMER.
YOU CAN'T AFFORD THAT. DO YOU KNOW THE MARKET VALUE FOR A WALKING DEAD?

MARKET VALUE?!
JESUS CHRIST, MAGGIE... DO YOU HEAR YOURSELF?

DON'T YOU MEAN, "JESUS CHRIST, MADAM PRESIDENT"?
...

YOU KNOW I HATE BEING CALLED THAT.
NOT IN THE MOOD FOR JOKES?

CARL, LOOK... I'M AS WORRIED AS YOU ARE HOW... CASUAL THINGS ARE GETTING. OUR PEOPLE, ALL ACROSS THE COLONIES, ARE GETTING SOFT.
AS OUR SAFE ZONE EXPANDS... AND ON THE EVE OF US LINKING UP WITH THE WESTERN ALLIANCE... MAYBE THIS IS HOW THINGS ARE SUPPOSED TO BE? MAYBE WE'VE EARNED THIS.
AT LEAST... THAT'S WHAT I TELL MYSELF.

I DON'T CARE WHAT YOU HAVE TO TELL YOURSELF. I KNOW YOU KNOW JUST AS WELL AS I DO THAT CARTING AROUND THOSE THINGS... BRINGING THEM INTO TOWN... IT'S DANGEROUS.
IT'S ONLY A MATTER OF TIME UNTIL YOUR SON GETS SOMEONE KILLED.
HOW MANY YEARS HAS IT BEEN SINCE SOMEONE WAS BITTEN? YOU WANT TO BRING THAT BACK?

CARL.

THAT'S NOT OUR WORLD ANYMORE. THAT'S ALL BEHIND US NOW. AM I SAYING NO ONE WILL EVER BE BITTEN AGAIN? NO... I'M SURE IT'LL HAPPEN, BUT THAT DOESN'T MEAN THINGS GO BACK TO HOW THEY WERE.
YOU NEED TO LET GO... FOR YOUR OWN SAKE. LIVE YOUR LIFE AND BE HAPPY. ENJOY THE WORLD YOUR FATHER HELPED MAKE FOR YOU... FOR ALL OF US.
STOP LOOKING FOR DANGER AROUND EVERY CORNER. IT'S JUST NOT THERE ANYMORE.

THIS WORLD DOESN'T LAST UNLESS WE ALL DO OUR PART TO KEEP IT GOING.
PARADING THE DEAD AROUND IN FRONT OF CHILDREN ISN'T WHAT MY DAD DIED FOR.

I MADE THIS EASY ON YOU, CARL. DON'T DO SOMETHING STUPID. ON YOUR NEXT RUN--BRING ONE OF THOSE THINGS BACK FOR HERSHEL.
DON'T MAKE THINGS WORSE!
DON'T WORRY ABOUT HIM.

THE ONE YOU SHOULD BE WORRIED ABOUT IS THAT SON OF YOURS.
YOU ALWAYS GAVE HIM WHATEVER HE WANTED... AND YOU STILL COME RUNNING IF THERE'S EVEN A HINT OF TROUBLE FOR HIM.
CAN YOU BLAME ME? AFTER EVERYTHING I SAW YOU LIVE THROUGH... I WANTED TO MAKE THINGS BETTER FOR HIM.

WELL, YOU CERTAINLY DID THAT... BUT I FEEL LIKE HE'D BE BETTER OFF IF YOU'D TOLD THE ASSHOLE "NO" EVERY ONCE IN A WHILE.

DON'T TALK ABOUT YOUR BROTHER LIKE THAT.
IN CASE YOU DON'T KNOW... EVERYONE TALKS ABOUT MY BROTHER LIKE THAT.
EVERYONE.

YOU'RE GOING TO END UP WITH A SEBASTIAN MILTON IF YOU'RE NOT CAREFUL. CARL IS THE LEAST OF YOUR WORRIES.

...

SLOW DOWN! SLOW DOWN!
I'M ON YOUR SIDE.

I KNOW. SOMETIMES I JUST WISH YOU WEREN'T THE ONLY ONE.

WHAT?
I'M NOT ENOUGH FOR YOU?

I'D SAY YOU'RE ALMOST TOO MUCH.
RACE TO ANDREA'S SCHOOL?

SURE... IF YOU WANT TO LOSE SOMETHING ELSE TODAY, FINE WITH ME.

ANDREA'S OUT. SHE'S WORRIED ABOUT YOU.
SHE SAID, "WHY IS DADDY SO MAD?"
I'LL TALK TO HER TOMORROW BEFORE I GO. I DON'T WANT HER TO WORRY.
READY FOR BED?

I'M GOING TO GO OUT... I NEED TO CLEAR MY HEAD BEFORE MY TRIP TOMORROW.

OH... OKAY.
HOW LATE WILL YOU BE?

I DON'T KNOW...

HERSHEL! YOU NEED TO SETTLE UP IF YOU'RE CHECKING OUT.
YOU KNOW MY FAMILY'S GOOD FOR IT. WE'LL SETTLE UP ON MY WAY BACK THROUGH TOWN.
COOL?

...

THANKS. I'LL BE SURE TO PATRONIZE YOUR BUSINESS AGAIN IN THE FUTURE.
MIGHT EVEN TALK MY MOM INTO STAYING HERE.

HERSHEL! HERSHEL!
COME QUICK!

I JUST WANTED... ONE LAST LOOK BEFORE YOU LEFT... BUT...

BYE, DADDY! I LOVE YOU!
I LOVE YOU, TOO!
I'LL BE HOME AS SOON AS I CAN.

YOU SURE THAT'S THE WHOLE LIST? I'VE NEVER SEEN YOU LOAD A CART SO FAST.
I'M IN A BIT OF A HURRY.

YOU THOUGHT YOU COULD SNEAK AWAY?

I CAME TO HELP YOU LOAD UP-- THEY SAID I'D JUST MISSED YOU.
YOU'RE NOT TRYING TO *AVOID* ME AGAIN, ARE YOU?

SORRY, LYDIA.
I NEEDED TO GET OUT OF TOWN IN A HURRY. I'LL TELL YOU ALL ABOUT IT ON THE ROAD.

SO... WHAT HAPPENS WHEN YOU GO BACK?
AFTER WHAT I DID? I HAVE NO IDEA.
NOTHING GOOD.
THE CRAZY THING IS I HAVE NO REGRETS. THAT MAY CHANGE DURING THIS TRIP... AS WE GET CLOSER AND CLOSER TO GOING BACK. BUT FOR NOW AT LEAST, I **KNOW** I DID THE RIGHT THING.

OF COURSE YOU DID. YOU ALWAYS HAVE.
THAT'S THE CARL GRIMES I KNOW.

OKAY, BACK TO IT. WHAT ABOUT JESUS AND AARON? ARE WE GOING ALL THE WAY DOWN RIVER?
NO. SOMEONE'S MEETING US ON THE BANK... **HERE.** IN FIVE DAYS.

THAT'LL TAKE NO MORE THAN THREE DAYS TO GET THERE. WE HITTING THE GROVES FIRST? NO... WE SHOULD SAVE THAT FOR THE WAY BACK SO WE CAN BRING THINGS HOME.
IF WE SWING THROUGH HERE... WE CAN MAKE A DROP WITH SPRINGHAVEN ON THE WAY.

SPRINGHAVEN? THROUGH ***THERE?*** THAT'S THE LONG WAY, TO PUT IT MILDLY.
WHY WOULD WE-- OH.

I DON'T KNOW WHY YOU EVEN BOTHER. HE'S ***NEVER*** THERE.
THE SUPPLIES ARE GETTING USED.
SOMEONE IS STAYING IN THE AREA-- EVEN IF THEY'RE HIDING FROM US.
FOR SOME REASON...
I CAN THINK OF A REASON OR TWO.

LUCILLE

KNOCK! KNOCK!

KNOCK! KNOCK!

HELLO?!
ANYONE?!

LET'S GO.
SORRY.
LUCILLE

I DON'T KNOW, MAYBE IT'S WEIRD... IT'S JUST NICE TO TALK TO ANYONE WHO KNEW HIM. Y'KNOW?
THERE'S THIS UNSPOKEN THING... THIS SENSE OF "YOU WERE THERE, YOU KNOW". HE'S NOT JUST A MYTH TO THEM.
HE'S REAL. IT... KEEPS HIM REAL FOR ME.

PLEASE TELL JESUS AND AARON I SAID HELLO.
THEY TOLD ME TO BEG YOU TO COME FOR A VISIT. THEY HAVEN'T SEEN ANDREA IN ABOUT A YEAR. THEY DID SAY THEY'LL COME TO YOU AS SOON AS THE HARVEST IS OVER.

WAIT, CARL... NO CARVINGS? LAUREN HAS BEEN ASKING ABOUT SOME WALRUS YOU SAID YOU'D MAKE HER FOR THE LAST TWO DROP-OFFS.
SHIT. I'M SO SORRY, ELIAS. I'VE JUST BEEN SO BUSY IT'S SLIPPED MY MIND. I HAVEN'T BEEN DOING MUCH CARVING LATELY.

WHAT'S THAT SOUND?
WHOA. HOLD UP.

...

THIS IS AMAZING.
I READ ABOUT THIS ONCE. HOW WHEN SETTLERS FIRST CAME TO THIS COUNTRY, THEY COULD HUNT BY BLINDLY FIRING THEIR GUNS INTO THE AIR WHEN A FLOCK PASSED OVERHEAD BECAUSE THE BIRD POPULATION WAS SO DENSE.
WE BROUGHT THE POPULATION DOWN... I GUESS THERE'S NOT ENOUGH OF US LEFT TO DO THAT.

I CAN'T BELIEVE YOU STILL WEAR THAT.
DAMN THING MUST BE WORTH A *FORTUNE.* I CAN'T BELIEVE YOU HAVEN'T ASKED FOR IT BACK.

A GIFT'S A GIFT.
WAS A TIME YOU NEEDED IT. IT MADE ME FEEL SAFE, THOUGHT IT'D MAKE YOU FEEL THE SAME.

I HOPE IT *STILL* MAKES YOU FEEL SAFE.

...

IT'S GOING TO BE COLD TONIGHT.
WE CAN *BOTH* SLEEP IN THE TENT.

I DON'T THINK SOPHIA WOULD APPRECIATE THAT.
HOW WOULD SHE FIND OUT?

I DON'T THINK *CONNER* WOULD APPRECIATE IT *EITHER.*

YOU KNOW... I WAS JUST JOKING AROUND. I'M NOT GOING TO TRY AND FUCK YOU.
I JUST DON'T WANT YOU HANGING OUT HERE... FREEZING ALL NIGHT. I WAS TRYING TO BE *NICE.*

...

OH MY GOD-- YOU SLEEP WITH IT ON, TOO?
WHAT?

THE EYE PATCH.
GOOD NIGHT.

I NEVER MADE YOU HIDE YOUR WOUND. I CELEBRATED IT WHEN WE WERE TOGETHER. I LOVED YOU BECAUSE OF IT, NOT IN SPITE OF IT. I WOULD HAVE NEVER ASKED YOU TO COVER IT UP.
REMEMBER HOW I USED TO LICK--

STOP IT.
I DON'T DO THIS FOR SOPHIA. SHE DOESN'T MAKE ME WEAR THIS. I DO IT FOR ANDREA.

SHE DOESN'T KNOW WHAT LIFE WAS LIKE... AND I DON'T WANT HER TO. I DON'T WANT HER TO LIVE IN A WORLD WHERE OUR SCARS ARE EXPOSED FOR EVERYONE TO SEE. I WANT A BETTER WORLD FOR HER.
SOUNDS LIKE YOU WANT TO LIE TO HER.

YOU LOOK AT MY FACE AND YOU SEE DEATH! I KNOW IT AND YOU KNOW IT. THAT'S THE WORLD I'M FROM--THAT WE'RE FROM! BUT THAT WORLD IS GONE--AND I DON'T WANT TO REMIND MY DAUGHTER OF IT EVERY TIME SHE LOOKS AT ME.
IT HAS NOTHING TO DO WITH ME OR SOPHIA OR YOU!
SO DROP IT!

I'M SORRY.

I'M SORRY ABOUT LAST NIGHT.
IT'S OKAY. JUST HURRY.
WE NEED TO GET THE CART LOADED AND TIED DOWN BEFORE THE TRAIN LEAVES THE STATION.

TRADE DEAL IMMINENT
EAST AND WEST TO FINALLY UNITE

OKAY, EVERYONE OUT! THIS IS AS FAR WEST AS THE TRAIN GOES--
FOR NOW.

OH MY GOD...
HE'S REALLY GOING TO DO IT.

WELCOME TO THE *WESTERN FRONT!*
DID YOU BRING THAT GRADING ATTACHMENT? PROGRESS HAS BEEN REALLY STALLED SINCE OURS BROKE.

I GOT YOUR LETTER. WE BROUGHT THE WHOLE LIST. I MEAN... WHO ARE YOU TALKING TO HERE?
I SHOULD NEVER HAVE DOUBTED YOU. YOU'RE THE BEST MESSENGER IN THE COMMONWEALTH, CARL.

AND HE DOES IT ALL BY HIMSELF.
I CAN'T BELIEVE HOW FAR YOU'VE COME SINCE LAST I WAS HERE. THE TRAIN JUST KEPT GOING AND GOING. IT'S *REMARKABLE.*

I KNOW, RIGHT? WE'LL HAVE MET THE WESTERN ALLIANCE'S TRACKS WITHIN A YEAR, FOR SURE--UNITING THE EAST AND WEST FOR THE FIRST TIME SINCE *THE TRIALS* FIRST BEGAN.
I JUST WISH STEPHANIE HAD LIVED TO SEE IT...
GOD, I HOPE I LIVE TO SEE IT THE WAY THINGS HAVE BEEN WITH ME LATELY.

OH, NONSENSE, EUGENE. YOU'RE AS HEALTHY AS A HORSE.
YEAH, A *SICK* ONE.

BUT ENOUGH ABOUT *THAT.* LET'S GET YOUR CART UNLOADED AND GET YOU FED.
COME ON.

YOU THINK HE'S REALLY SICK?
HE'S BEEN TALKING LIKE THAT FOR YEARS.
BUT REALLY... I DON'T KNOW. UH...

LET ME...
NO. IT'S OKAY. I'LL BE FINE.
I'LL CATCH UP TO YOU.

...
I DIDN'T KNOW YOU WERE WORKING OUT HERE.

ONE OF THE LAST PLACES LEFT THAT ACTUALLY NEEDS SECURITY... AND EVEN STILL WE DON'T SEE MUCH ACTION.
I PREFER THE OUTER TERRITORIES... LESS RICK GRIMES WORSHIP GOING ON OUT HERE. PEOPLE ARE TOO BUSY TO PRAISE YOUR FATHER FOR SHIT HE HAD ALMOST NOTHING TO DO WITH.

NICE SEEING YOU, TOO, LAURA.

I'M NEVER GOING TO FORGET WHAT HE DID.

...

YOU KNOW WHAT? I WAS WITH MY FATHER A WHOLE LOT LONGER THAN YOU WERE. I WAS A KID, BUT HEARD WAY MORE THAN ANYONE THOUGHT I DID... AND YOU KNOW WHAT?
DWIGHT WAS FAR FROM THE ONLY PERSON WHO DIED ALONG THE WAY... THERE ARE MANY PEOPLE WHO ARE DEAD BECAUSE OF RICK GRIMES.
BUT EVERY SINGLE PERSON ALIVE TODAY... IS ALIVE BECAUSE OF HIM. INCLUDING YOU!

...

YOU KNOW WHY THINGS ARE QUIET... EVEN OUT HERE? HIM.
SHOW A LITTLE RESPECT.

LOOKING FORWARD TO HEADING BACK TOMORROW?
AFTER THAT?
WITH WHAT I'M UP AGAINST BACK HOME?
MAYBE A LITTLE.

HERE'S YOUR CUT.
...
LYDIA... YOU'RE A GOOD FRIEND.
I KNOW.
I LOVE YOU, TOO.

DADDY!

ANDREA! COME HERE, GIRL!
I MISSED YOU BUNCHES AND BUNCHES AND BUNCHES!

IT WAS THE BIGGEST SNAKE I EVER SAW. I THINK IT WAS A MILE LONG! MOMMY KILLED IT DEAD!
REALLY?! WOW... THAT'S REALLY... THAT'S...
I'M GOING TO NEED YOU TO RUN ON INTO THE HOUSE WHILE I TALK TO YOUR MOMMY.

YEAH... I THINK THAT'D BE BEST.

IS MOMMY MAD?
NO MORE THAN SHE SHOULD BE.
RUN ALONG.

WHY, GODDAMN IT? JUST TELL ME WHY!
YOU WERE REALLY THAT MAD? OVER SOME STUPID TRAVELING SIDESHOW?! THEY'RE GOING TO ARREST YOU OVER THIS!
WHY?!

IF I GO TO JAIL... OKAY.
I MADE A SACRIFICE TO KEEP MY DAUGHTER SAFE. THAT'S WHAT MY DAD TAUGHT ME.

ANDREA WAS SAFE-- SHE IS SAFE!
SHE'LL BE LESS SAFE WITHOUT YOU!

...

FASTER THAN I THOUGHT THEY'D BE...
DAMN IT.

I'M NOT REALLY GETTING A FUGITIVE VIBE FROM YOU. I COULD TAKE THE CUFFS OFF AND THEN PUT THEM BACK ON BEFORE WE ARRIVE AT THE STATION.
MISTER GRIMES, I FEEL BAD ABOUT ALL THIS...
IT'S FINE. DON'T WORRY ABOUT IT.

FOR THE RECORD... I DON'T FAULT YOU AT ALL FOR WHAT YOU DID. KEEPING THOSE THINGS AS PETS IS DANGEROUS.
SHOULD BE OUTLAWED NO MATTER WHO IS DOING IT... IF YOU GET WHAT I'M SAYING.

YEAH. I DO.
THANKS.

GOING ALL THE WAY TO COMMONWEALTH ONE TO BE SEEN BY JUDGE HAWTHORNE... YOU REALLY PISSED OFF THE PRESIDENT WITH THIS ONE.
STILL... NOT THE WAY A GRIMES SHOULD BE TREATED. WHOLE MESS OF PEOPLE ARE REALLY ANGRY ABOUT THIS.

YEAH?

FIVE MINUTES, I MEAN IT.
OKAY. THANKS.

I'M SORRY ABOUT BEFORE.
DON'T BE. YOU HAVE EVERY RIGHT TO BE ANGRY. I'VE BEEN... STUPID.

YES, YOU HAVE.
BUT LISTEN... IT'S STILL AN INFORMAL HEARING. SO THINGS COULD BE WORSE. THERE'S THE DESTRUCTION OF PROPERTY CHARGE... BUT HERSHEL IS NOW CLAIMING HE TOOK THE WHOLE THING AS A THREAT... ON HIS LIFE.

THAT'S ABSURD.
I KNOW... BUT IT'S COMPLICATING THINGS. I THINK THAT'S WHY IT GOT KICKED UP TO THE HIGH COURT SO QUICKLY.

YEAH... THAT WORRIED ME.
JUDGE HAWTHORNE, THOUGH... THAT'S GOTTA BE A GOOD THING, RIGHT?

I DON'T KNOW...
I HOPE SO.

ALL RISE FOR THE HONORABLE JUDGE HAWTHORNE.

YOU MAY BE SEATED.

I'M NOT GOING TO BOTHER RESTATING THE ISSUES WE'RE HERE TO ADDRESS. IT'S ALL ANYONE HAS BEEN TALKING ABOUT FOR DAYS... "CARL GRIMES ON TRIAL".
SO I MUST REMIND YOU... THIS IS NOT A TRIAL. THIS IS AN INFORMAL HEARING... AND THIS IS THE HIGH COURT.
THAT MEANS WHEN I MAKE MY RULING, IT IS FINAL... AND I ALONE RULE AGAINST THE ACCUSED. NO JURY. NO LAWYERS. NO TRIAL.

THESE HEARINGS ARE MEANT TO BE SWIFT... SO IN THE INTEREST OF STAYING TRUE TO THEIR DESIGN... MISTER GRIMES... LET'S HEAR WHAT YOU HAVE TO SAY IN YOUR DEFENSE.

THANK YOU, MICH--
JUDGE HAWTHORNE.
I AM NOT IGNORANT TO THE LAWS THAT GOVERN THE CITIZENS OF THE COMMONWEALTH. I KNOW HOW IMPORTANT PERSONAL PROPERTY IS TO US ALL... AND HOW SEVERE A CRIME DESTROYING SAID PROPERTY IS.

BUT WHEN THAT CREATURE WALKED ACROSS MY LAND... I DIDN'T SEE A FINE PIECE OF FURNITURE, OR VALUABLE LIVESTOCK, OR A BEAUTIFUL FRUIT TREE.
I SAW THE THING THAT TOOK SO MANY OF OUR LIVES... SOME RIGHT IN FRONT OF ME.
AND I DID WHAT I KNEW HAD TO BE DONE.

I WAS THEN ORDERED TO REPLACE THE ROAMER I'D KILLED. IT'S ONE THING TO WORRY ONE OF HERSHEL'S PETS MIGHT ATTACK SOMEONE... I COULDN'T BEAR THE THOUGHT OF IT BEING ONE I PROVIDED HIM.
THE THOUGHT OF THAT... IT PUSHED ME OVER THE EDGE...

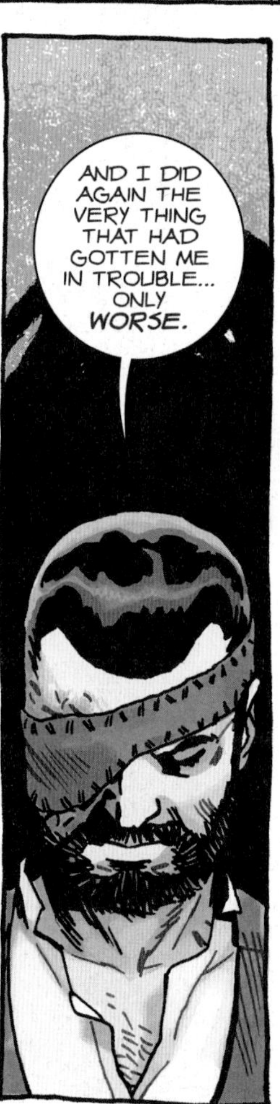
AND I DID AGAIN THE VERY THING THAT HAD GOTTEN ME IN TROUBLE... ONLY WORSE.

THE THING IS... I KNEW THEY WERE THERE. I KNEW THEY WERE DANGEROUS. IT WAS SOMETHING I FELT I HAD TO DO.
MAYBE I'M A RELIC. MAYBE I DON'T LOOK AT THE WORLD THE RIGHT WAY... MAYBE I'M NOT... ADJUSTED WELL ENOUGH TO THIS NEW WORLD.

I'M A MESSENGER. I SPEND WEEKS AT A TIME OUT ON THE ROAD, OFTEN FAR OUTSIDE THE SAFE ZONE... WHERE THINGS ARE ALMOST AS BAD AS THEY WERE.
SO THE DANGERS AREN'T SO FAR IN THE PAST THAT THEY'RE EASILY FORGOTTEN... NOT FOR ME.

AND...
I HAVE A DAUGHTER.

SHE MEANS EVERYTHING TO ME. ANDREA IS STRONG, CONFIDENT... AND BRILLIANT.

EVERY BIT AS MUCH AS HER NAMESAKE.

I SEE THE WAY SHE LOOKS AT THE WORLD, WIDE-EYED AND FULL OF... OPTIMISM... AND I WANT TO KEEP THAT. I DON'T EVER WANT THAT TO CHANGE.

ANDREA IS SIX YEARS OLD, AND SHE'S NEVER EVEN SEEN A ROAMER.
THAT'S THE WORLD MY FATHER BUILT. THAT'S THE WORLD WE SHOULD ALL BE WORKING OUR HARDEST TO MAINTAIN.

BUT I'M HERE, DEFENDING MYSELF FOR KILLING SOMETHING THAT SHOULD BE EXTERMINATED.
HAVE YOU FORGOTTEN HOW THINGS ARE OUTSIDE THE SAFE ZONE? HOW EASILY WE CAN FALL BACK TO THE OLD WAYS?

THIS IS JUST...
IT'S...
THAT'S ALL I HAVE TO SAY.

YOU BRING UP A GOOD POINT, CARL GRIMES, ONE OF THE HEROES OF THE TRIALS, SON OF THE GREAT RICK GRIMES.
PEOPLE DON'T SEEM TO REMEMBER HOW THINGS WERE. IT'S TRUE. EVEN I HAVE TO SOMETIMES REMIND MYSELF THAT SOME OF THE THINGS I LIVED THROUGH ACTUALLY HAPPENED.
THAT'S HOW PEACEFUL THINGS ARE NOW, IN GENERAL, THAT IT MAKES IT HARD TO REMEMBER WHAT WE'VE OVERCOME... OR EVEN THE TIME BEFORE THE TRIALS.
I'M REMINDED OF THE WORDS ON THE BASE OF A CERTAIN STATUE YOU ALL HAD TO WALK PAST TO GET INTO THIS BUILDING.
LAND THAT WE

"HOW MANY HOURS ARE IN A DAY WHEN YOU DON'T SPEND HALF OF THEM WATCHING TELEVISION?
"WHEN IS THE LAST TIME ANY OF US REALLY WORKED TO GET SOMETHING THAT WE WANTED?
"HOW LONG HAS IT BEEN SINCE ANY OF US HAS REALLY NEEDED SOMETHING THAT WE WANTED?
"THE WORLD WE KNEW IS GONE.

"THE WORLD OF COMMERCE AND FRIVOLOUS NECESSITY HAS BEEN REPLACED BY A WORLD OF SURVIVAL AND RESPONSIBILITY.

"AN EPIDEMIC OF APOCALYPTIC PROPORTIONS HAS SWEPT THE GLOBE, CAUSING THE DEAD TO RISE AND FEED ON THE LIVING.

"IN A MATTER OF MONTHS SOCIETY HAS CRUMBLED, NO GOVERNMENT, NO GROCERY STORES, NO MAIL DELIVERY, NO CABLE TV.

"IN A WORLD RULED BY THE DEAD, WE ARE FORCED TO FINALLY START LIVING."

IT'S THAT LAST LINE THAT'S MOST IMPORTANT TO ME... BECAUSE THEY'RE BASICALLY SAYING THAT THE TRIALS WE LIVED THROUGH... GAVE US A BETTER WORLD THAN THE ONE WE HAD BEFORE.
THAT INVOLVED A LOT OF SACRIFICE, SO THAT'S AN UNPOPULAR INTERPRETATION, BUT I KNOW PEOPLE WHO AGREE WITH ME. THE WORLD WE LIVE IN NOW IS QUIETER, SIMPLER, MORE FAIR... MORE JUST... AND HAPPIER.
THE DEAD MADE US LIVE.
BUT, OH, WHAT WE GAVE UP TO GET HERE... LET US NEVER FORGET, SO THAT WE CAN HONOR THOSE WHO WE LOST ALONG THE WAY.

THE OWNING AND DISPLAYING OF ROAMERS FOR PROFIT IS AN ABHORRENT PRACTICE. I'VE ALWAYS FELT THAT WAY.
IT IS THE BEST EXAMPLE OF FORGETTING WHAT WE'VE LIVED THROUGH AND DISHONORING THOSE WE HAVE LOST. THAT IS WHY I'M PUTTING FORTH A MOTION TO OUTLAW IT THROUGHOUT THE COMMONWEALTH.
THIS MATTER IS SETTLED.

MISTER GRIMES, YOU'RE FREE TO GO.

SO THAT'S IT?
YEAH... THAT'S IT. HIGH COURT. BOOM.

DID YOU REALLY THINK I WAS GOING TO LET THEM SEND ONE OF MY FAVORITE PEOPLE TO JAIL?

I MEAN... IT WAS MY SWORD YOU USED!
YOU TAKING GOOD CARE OF IT?

I KEEP IT NICE AND SHARP... JUST IN CASE.
I DON'T THINK THERE ARE MANY PEOPLE WHO WOULD BELIEVE THE FAMOUS JUDGE HAWTHORNE USED TO CARRY A SWORD.

SHE DIDN'T.
IT WAS MICHONNE WHO CARRIED THE SWORD.

MICHONNE WAS SOMEONE WHO CARRIED A LOT OF GUILT. IT HAUNTED HER... HAD HER TALKING TO GHOSTS, PUSHING PEOPLE AWAY, AND FORGETTING WHO SHE *WAS.*
HAWTHORNE WAS MY EX-HUSBAND'S NAME. I NEVER CHANGED IT AFTER THE DIVORCE BECAUSE MY PRACTICE KNEW ME UNDER THAT NAME.
EVENTUALLY... THAT NAME WAS JUST A PAINFUL REMINDER OF A FAILED MARRIAGE AND *LOST* CHILDREN. SO I HID FROM IT... AND WHO I WAS.

NOW? I FEEL LIKE I EARNED IT BACK, THE WORK I'VE DONE... WHAT I'VE ACCOMPLISHED. IT'S WHO I AM NOW.
I NEVER WOULD HAVE BEEN ABLE TO DO THAT WITHOUT YOUR FATHER... AND THE WORLD *HE* BUILT.
THERE ARE SOME PEOPLE OUT THERE WHO FEEL LIKE YOUR FATHER GETS TOO MUCH CREDIT. THERE WERE SO MANY OF US *HELPING* HIM ALONG THE WAY.
SURE.

BUT I FEEL LIKE HE STILL DOESN'T GET *ENOUGH* CREDIT.
SO ANY TIME I HAVE A CHANCE TO SET SOMETHING RIGHT OR HONOR THE MAN IN SOME SMALL WAY--*I TAKE IT.*
LUCKY FOR ME.

I'VE MISSED YOU, CARL. YOU NEED TO COME VISIT MORE OFTEN... AND UNDER BETTER CIRCUMSTANCES.
AND, *JESUS*-- ANDREA IS *SIX* ALREADY?

YEP.

MY WORD... TIME JUST KEEPS DOING WHAT TIME DOES, DOESN'T IT?
NOW THAT THINGS ARE CALM ENOUGH TO LET IT...
YEAH.

I'M NOT WHO YOU THINK I AM...

HERSHEL, YOU...
SHOULDN'T BE SNEAKING UP ON ME LIKE THAT.

I'M NOT SOME SPOILED BRAT WHO GOT WHATEVER HE WANTED AND THINKS HE'S ABOVE THE LAW.
I BUILT A BUSINESS... I PROVIDED A SERVICE.

IF YOU GET YOUR WAY, PEOPLE WILL FORGET HOW THINGS WERE. YOU'LL SEE.
MY SHOW REMINDED THEM WHAT WAS OUT THERE. KEPT THEM AFRAID... MADE THEM APPRECIATE WHAT THEY HAVE.

I NEVER MET MY FATHER. ALMOST NO ONE REMEMBERS HIM. NO ONE BUILDS STATUES OF HIM OR WRITES BOOKS ABOUT WHAT HE DID.
MOST OF WHAT I KNOW ABOUT HIM IS INSIDE ME. WHO I AM... TELLS ME WHO HE WAS. WHEN I FELT THE FEAR OF BEING AROUND THOSE THINGS... I FELT LIKE I WAS FEELING WHAT HE FELT.
IT FELT LIKE I WAS GETTING CLOSER TO HIM.

FUCK YOU FOR WHAT YOU DID.

...

HOWDY, STRANGER.

HEY.
"HEY"? I REALLY THOUGHT YOU'D BE IN A BETTER MOOD.

IT'S LIKE I DON'T KNOW YOU AT ALL.
SORRY. I'M HAPPY. RELIEVED. WE CAN GO HOME AND CELEBRATE. I'M JUST...

I KNOW. IT'S BEEN A LONG FEW DAYS.
WHOA, DUDE-- NICE EYE PATCH! YOU LEAVE THE PARROT AT HOME?
MAYBE HE ATE IT... FUCKING SAVAGE, THIS GUY.

HEY, GUYS! STOP IT!
DON'T YOU REALIZE WHO THIS IS? THIS IS CARL GRIMES. HE LIVED THROUGH THE TRIALS! THAT MEANS HE MADE SACRIFICES SO THAT WE COULD HAVE WHAT WE HAVE.
MY DAD TOLD ME ALL ABOUT IT.

HUH? UM... WHAT-EVER.
SORRY, MISTER GRIMES... THEY DIDN'T MEAN NOTHING.

IT'LL PROBABLY BE ANOTHER GENERATION BEFORE PEOPLE START REALLY TAKING THIS ALL FOR GRANTED.

IT WASN'T LIKE THIS, YOU KNOW? THE CHEST ALL PUFFED OUT--HE LOOKS LIKE HE'S CALLING DOWN A STORM FROM THE HEAVENS OR SOMETHING.
IT'S HOW PEOPLE *WANT* TO REMEMBER HIM.

THE MAN WHO MADE THE WORLD.
YEAH.

IT'S JUST... HE DID ENOUGH THAT YOU SHOULDN'T *HAVE* TO FAKE IT.

IT'S JUST A STATUE, CARL.
LET'S GO HOME SO YOU DON'T HAVE TO LOOK AT IT ANYMORE.

DID YOU EVER THINK WE'D MAKE IT HERE?
HERE? TO THIS FARM HOUSE? NO. OF COURSE NOT.
YOU KNOW WHAT I MEAN.

THIS IS WHAT I'M THINKING ABOUT WHEN I SAY MY DAD DOESN'T GET ENOUGH CREDIT... THAT THEY DON'T NEED TO CHANGE HIS STATUE SO HE LOOKS... COOLER.
JUST LOOK AT US. LOOK AT THIS PLACE. LOOK AT WHAT WE HAVE. WHAT OUR LIVES ARE.

I KNOW. I KNOW. I HAVEN'T BEEN SCARED, REALLY SCARED IN... I CAN'T EVEN REMEMBER.
DO YOU THINK THERE WAS EVER A TIME WHEN PEOPLE APPRECIATED WHAT THEY HAVE MORE THAN WE DO NOW?

ALL I KNOW IS I *REALLY* APPRECIATE WHAT I HAVE.
I LOVE YOU, CARL GRIMES.

DADDY!
DADDY!

WILL YOU READ TO ME BEFORE BED?

YOU JUST WANT TO STAY UP LATER, ANDREA. YOU THINK I DON'T SEE THROUGH THIS?

COME ON...

DO NOT FEAR, DEAR READER, FOR THIS MAY SEEM LIKE A SCARY BOOK AT FIRST, AND YOUR MOMMY OR DADDY MAY EVEN READ IT IN A SCARY VOICE.
SHAME ON THEM.
BUT THIS IS NOT A SCARY STORY. THIS IS A STORY ABOUT HOPE.

ONE DAY, A LONG TIME AGO, DEAD PEOPLE DECIDED THEY DIDN'T WANT TO BE DEAD ANYMORE.
NOBODY KNOWS WHY. AND DON'T BE EMBARRASSED, IT SCARED EVERYONE.
NOBODY KNEW WHAT WAS HAPPENING, OR WHY... BUT LIFE CHANGED.

EVERYONE WAS TESTED. THAT'S WHY THIS TIME CAME TO BE CALLED THE TRIALS.
YOU'VE PROBABLY HEARD YOUR PARENTS TALK ABOUT IT.
IT WAS A SCARY TIME, AND MANY GOOD, STRONG PEOPLE LOST THEMSELVES ALONG THE WAY.

THEY STARTED TO FORGET WHO THEY WERE, THEY EVEN STARTED TO FORGET WHAT WAS GOOD AND BAD.
THEY ONLY WORRIED ABOUT LIVING. THERE WAS NO TIME TO FOLLOW THE RULES.
ALMOST NOBODY BRUSHED THEIR TEETH OR WENT TO SLEEP BY THEIR BEDTIME.

A GREAT DARKNESS FELL ACROSS THE WHOLE WORLD. IT MADE EVERYONE SAD.
PEOPLE DIDN'T KNOW IF THINGS WOULD EVER GET BACK TO NORMAL.
MOST PEOPLE WERE SURE IT NEVER WOULD... AND THEY GOT SADDER... AND MEANER.

WHEN THINGS WERE AT THEIR DARKEST... A MAN CAME ALONG. SOMEONE WHO HAD BEEN HURT BY THE TRIALS.
BUT HE DIDN'T LET IT MAKE HIM SAD.
NOT ALL THE TIME AT LEAST, AND WE ALL KNOW IT'S OKAY TO BE SAD SOMETIMES.

RICK GRIMES HAD AN IDEA. HE KNEW THAT IF WE STAYED TOGETHER AND MADE FRIENDS INSTEAD OF ENEMIES... WE COULD DO ANYTHING.
EVEN REMAKE THE WORLD.

HE MADE FRIENDS AND LOST FRIENDS AS HE MOVED ACROSS THE COUNTRY. HE MET PEOPLE HE THOUGHT WOULD BE FRIENDS, BUT THEY TURNED OUT TO BE BAD.
HE SOMETIMES HAD TO HURT THE BAD PEOPLE TO PROTECT HIS FRIENDS.
SOMETIMES HE WAS SCARED THAT HE WAS BECOMING A BAD PERSON.

BUT HE NEVER DID.
AND HE TAUGHT OTHER PEOPLE HOW TO NOT LET THE TRIALS TURN THEM INTO BAD PEOPLE.
HE EVEN MET BAD PEOPLE AND TURNED THEM INTO FRIENDS.

RICK TRAVELED FAR AND WIDE, ALWAYS BRINGING HIS FRIENDS WITH HIM, AND THEY MADE HIM STRONGER.
THEY MADE HIM SAFE.
AND HE TAUGHT PEOPLE HOW TO MAKE FRIENDS AND USE THEM TO MAKE THEM STRONGER AND SAFER.

THE TRIALS MADE PEOPLE SO ANGRY THAT SOME OF THEM JUST WANTED TO *FIGHT.* BUT RICK KNEW THIS WAS *WRONG.*
HE SHOWED THEM HOW TO BE FRIENDS INSTEAD.
THE TRIALS WERE DANGEROUS TIMES... AND EVEN RICK DIDN'T SURVIVE THEM.

BUT HE WAS ABLE TO SHOW US THE WAY. WITH HIS TEACHINGS, THE TRIALS ENDED... AND LIFE RETURNED TO NORMAL.
RICK GRIMES
WE EVEN HAVE ICE CREAM AGAIN!
ANDREA GRIMES
PEOPLE ARE HAPPY INSTEAD OF SAD, AND SAFE INSTEAD OF SCARED, AND NICE INSTEAD OF MEAN. ALL BECAUSE SOMEONE WAS STRONG ENOUGH TO DO WHAT WAS RIGHT.
WHEREVER YOU ARE, WHATEVER YOU'RE DOING... YOU'RE THERE AND YOU'RE SAFE BECAUSE OF *RICK GRIMES.*

YOU WOULD HAVE REALLY LIKED HIM.

WHO?

YOUR GRAND-FATHER.

HE DID ALL THOSE THINGS, MY FATHER, YOUR GRANDFATHER.
RICK GRIMES.
THIS BOOK IS ABOUT *HIM.*

I *KNOW,* DAD!
YOU TELL ME THAT *EVERY* TIME.

READ IT AGAIN!

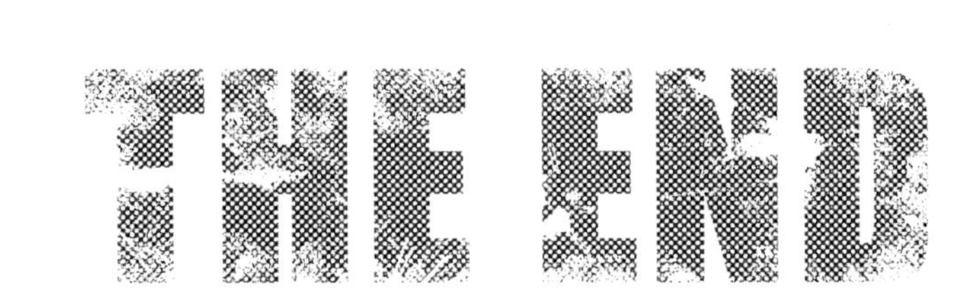
THE END

This is the end of THE WALKING DEAD.

That's it... it's over... we're done.

I'm sure you have a million questions... and I'm sure you feel as emotional about all this as we do... if not more so. I'm completely willing to bet some of you are angry over this. I get it... I do. I mean... WHY didn't we announce this so that fans would have some time to prepare?

Well... personally... I hate knowing what's coming. As a fan, I hate it when I realize I'm in the third act of a movie and the story is winding down. I hate that I can count commercial breaks and know I'm nearing the end of a TV show. I hate that you can FEEL when you're getting to the end of a book, or a graphic novel.

Some of the BEST episodes of *Game of Thrones* are when they're structured in such a way and paced to perfection so your brain can't tell if it's been watching for 15 minutes or 50 minutes... and when the end comes... you're STUNNED.

I love LONG movies for that very reason. You lose track of time because you went in convinced that you're going to be there for a long time, but the story moves at such an entertaining and engaging pace that by the time the movie's wrapping up... you can't believe it's already over. SURPRISE, it's over!

All I've ever done, all a creator can really do... is tailor-make stories to entertain themselves, and hope the audience feels the same way. That's all I've ever been doing... and it seems to work most of the time.

THE WALKING DEAD has always been built on surprise. Not knowing what's going to happen when you turn the page, who's going to die, how they're going to die... it's been ESSENTIAL to the success of this series. It's been the lifeblood that's been keeping it going all these years, keeping people engaged.

It just felt WRONG and against the very nature of this series not to make the actual end as surprising as all the big deaths... from Shane all the way to Rick.

To be honest... it seemed like a really good idea at the time, but now that we're here and the series is over, I'm having second thoughts. Not so much so that I'm changing course... that would be kind of impossible to do anyway. But... it's possible, as much as I hate to admit it, that I'm genuinely feeling a sense of regret over this whole crazy plan.

I want you to see what went into this though, I want you to understand why, if that's possible. I feel like you all deserve at least that. So let's pull the curtain back in a way... well, I usually try not to do. When it comes to the end of this series... here's how the sausage got made.

Way back in early 2015, Charlie Adlard turned in the cover for issue #142. He had taken my direction, of showing happy people at the Alexandria fair, the booths, the commerce... a very civilized scene, and he'd worked wonders with the concept. It was a cover unlike anything that had come before. To me, it was a real turning point for this series.

The thing is... this was over four years ago at this point... but I knew pretty much every big story point that was going to happen all the way up to this final issue. A couple years prior, around 2013 or so, I'd even told Charlie at San Diego Comic-Con what the gist of this final issue was. I revealed how the story would end with Carl reading his daughter a storybook about Rick's exploits. I just didn't know exactly what issue that story would fall in. I knew the end... but I didn't know where it would fall. I figured... somewhere past issue #300. As I've said publicly... I've always wanted to reach that number, that big, round *Cerebus* number that all the insane indy comics creators try to chase.

But when I saw the cover to #142... it dawned on me. "Oh, shit... we're already at the fair! The Commonwealth is just around the corner... and... oh, man... there's no WAY I'm going to make it to issue #300." It was the first time I realized that I just didn't have enough story worked out to get there. I didn't know exactly how long we'd fight the Whisperers or how long we'd be spending in the Commonwealth before Rick would bring about his own demise... but I knew the whole run wouldn't be another 150 issues.

I started working things out... trying to figure out how long things would run... and it dawned on me... I had about 50 issues until I got to my planned end. I always have to keep collections in mind. Now that we do 48-issue compendiums (that are very popular, our most popular format), it would be really irresponsible to wrap this series up in a way that resulted in compendium readers having to buy a different format to finish the series. So I was happy that it appeared things would work out where this series would wrap up nicely in the fourth compendium.

But I wasn't quite sure it was time to wrap things up.

I love writing this series. It's been my life's dream. So when I first came to this realization... my first instinct was, "Well, I just need to come up with more story". I even spent a few weeks trying to come up with new plot, new story detours to push the ending I had in mind back and keep things going... for a while, possibly even a long while... an extra compendium, maybe two.

And... again, pulling the curtain back... this has happened before. I'd already abandoned one planned ending to keep the series going. Yep... that's an exclusive I've never revealed anywhere.

Let's go off on a tangent for a moment. When the story got to Alexandria in issue #72, things were going to go pretty much as they did; Rick and his crew were going to have trouble fitting in because of everything they'd been through. That would lead to conflict within Alexandria, and it would eventually lead to Rick taking over. The big storyline NO WAY OUT ended with Rick proclaiming that Alexandria was a place worth fighting for, that they could no longer keep moving from place to place... they had to take a stand, lay down roots and start building from there. Their nomad days were behind them.

Well, for years... that had been planned to be... the end. Rick would make his proclamation, and the speech would end with a big close-up on Rick's face, you'd turn the page, and Rick's face would be the same, only it was a statue... and you'd zoom out and see the full statue with some vines growing on the bottom of it... cracks forming... and you'd realize that it was quite OLD.

We'd keep zooming out until we saw that the statue was in Alexandria, the same place where he gave the speech, but it was different. It was old and rundown, broken windows and missing doors. We would keep zooming out until a zombie walked by, then another... and we'd see that Rick had brought them to Alexandria, given this grand speech about rebuilding civilization and SUCCEEDED to the point that they built a statue to honor him... but in the end, the dead won, society crumbled again, this time seemingly for good... and that was it.

It was a TERRIBLE ending. Bleak, sad... made the whole story pointless. What can I say... I was young and most of the endings I wrote or came up with way back then... were pretty bleak. So that ending... in hindsight was embarrassingly bad, but more than that, I wasn't ready to end this series. Not by a long shot.

You have to understand, when I started writing this series, I had no clue I'd make it to issue #12. So the thought of having a book that ran 100 issues was insane. So when this book really took off in its second year, I was able to make far reaching plans for the future, but even at that point, a 100-issue run still seemed impossible.

So when I found myself staring down the barrel of a completed 100-issue series, I just wasn't ready to let go. I was having too much fun. Think about how things would have gone if I'd wrapped things up then... no Negan, no Ezekiel, no All Out War, no time jump, no Magna, no Whisperers, no Commonwealth, no Princess... and a really crummy ending to boot.

To top it off... shortly after I scrapped that planned ending and decided to keep going, I came up with pretty much the exact ending of this issue, which I felt was much more fitting and rewarding.

I'm glad I made the decision I did back then. I have no regrets.

This time though, things were very different. As I worked to come up with ways to expand the story, none of it felt right. Everything felt like an unnecessary detour... it was, for lack of a better word, filler. The harder I tried to come up with new places to go, the clearer it was to me that this is what this story needed... it needed to end.

So like I said... it seemed like a good idea at the time. FOUR YEARS ago this plan seemed rock solid. Never tell anyone, keep it secret, and even go as far as soliciting fake issues that will never exist so that we can really surprise people. Oh, man... I thought this was going to be great.

I worked it out with Charlie right away. He'd always been pushing to end on a high note. He was with me, all the way, as long as I didn't run this series into the ground. Charlie just wanted to make this book special. If I had a solid plan for 300 issues, he'd have made it happen, but if I started turning in stories

Charlie thought were lame... I would have heard about it and he'd have convinced me to end the series. So when we talked about the plan, Charlie was excited, his fear of us overstaying our welcome and keeping this book going well past its popularity were quelled.

I'll say it again, I love (loved... oh, god, I'm not ready for past tense) writing this series. I really don't want it to end. In fact, I've been... kind of unsettled since I wrote the script for this issue. The whole thing just feels... weird.

In a way, killing this series has been a lot like killing a major character. Much, much harder... but the same feeling. I don't WANT to do it. I'd rather keep going... but the story is telling me what it wants and what it needs. This needs to happen. Whether I want it or not.

It just feels right... while also feeling... terrible.

The main point of all this is... well, I'm scared. Most of my professional life has been spent on this series. Countless hours are dedicated to this, month in and month out. More than anything in the last 16 years... this is going to fundamentally change my life. So I'm terrified.

When my fingers typed out "THE END" on the keyboard as I finished this script... I thought I'd feel relief, or some sliver of pride in a job well done, but it was really just... dread. I wasn't ready for it to be over... but it was.

It is.

Oddly, as unsure as I feel about ending the story, I feel confident in how I ended it. I've been building to this for years, and it does feel good to end on such a happy note. To know that everything these characters lived through meant something. To see that Michonne got to find her daughter, find peace with her life, and even have a grandchild... that feels good. That the world is fixed... and at peace, that in some ways it's even better than before... that's meaningful. And to see Carl in that rocking chair, reading happily to his daughter, to know that's the life Rick wanted him to have... that makes me happy.

I hope it makes you happy, too. Even if you're upset at not getting to spend time in this world anymore.

I'm upset, too. I'm going to miss it as much as you will, if not more so. It breaks my heart that I had to end it, and we have to move on... but I just love this world too much to stretch things out until it doesn't live up to what I want it to be.

I hope you understand.

I hope you, dear reader, know how much I appreciate the gift you have given me. I got to tell my story exactly how I wanted to, for 193 issues, and end it on my terms, with no interference at all along the way... at any point. That's such a rare thing, and it doesn't exist without the unyielding support this series got from readers like you. Thank you so much.

Thank you, Tony Moore, for drawing the first six issues. Thank you, Cliff Rathburn, for countless hours spent shaping black and white art with gray tones. Thank you, Rus Wooton, for turning my words into art month after month. Thank you, Stefano Gaudiano, for shaping Charlie's pencils for nearly 100 issues. Thank you, Aubrey Sitterson and Sina Grace, for your time keeping this insanity in check. Thank you, Sean Mackiewicz, for seeing this project all the way to the end, despite thinking each compendium would be your last... and, y'know, doing a great job along the way. Thank you, Arielle Basich, for keeping Sean sane and doing the heavy lifting. Thank you, Andres Juarez, for keeping this book looking fresh after being on the shelf for over a decade. Thank you, Carina Taylor, for doing your part to do the same. Thank you, Dave Stewart, for making Charlie's art pop on comic shelves the world over. Thank you, Dave McCaig, for you know what. Thank you, Ryan Ottley, for that amazing art in issue #75 that may never get collected. Thank you, Cory Walker, for your wise council before I even started this series. Thank you, Jim Valentino, for so many things, including saying, "Change the title so you can own it". Thank you, Shawn Kirkham, for always having an ear to the ground for what this world needs. Thank you to the team at Skybound, who work tirelessly to bring you everything THE WALKING DEAD you could ever want and more. Thank you, Erik Larsen, for the undying support, even to this day. Thank you, Eric Stephenson, for the years of strategy sessions that made this series a continued success. Thank you to the evolving staff at Image Comics that was invaluable over the last decade and a half... especially the accounting department. Thank you, David Alpert, for your part in turning this into a truly worldwide, multi-media phenomenon, and all that came with it and somehow so much more than that. Thank you, Shep Rosenman and Lee Rosenbaum, for crossing the Ts and dotting the Is so I can keep all my Ts and not lose my Is. Thank you, Chris Simonian, for going to war and winning. Thank you, Allen Grodsky, for going to war and winning. Thank you, John Campisi and the team at CAA, for continuing the fight. Thank you, Frank Darabont, for going into House of Secrets in Burbank and saying, "This one." Thank you, Gale Anne Hurd, for helping turn "this one" into something real. Thank you, Charles H. Eglee, for being the original showrunner and setting us up for success. Thank you, Jack LoGiudice, for making me feel welcome in the writer's room on day one... by being mean to me in the most entertaining ways. Thank you, Glen Mazzara, for keeping the fire warm. Thank you, Scott Gimple, for taking the show to new heights and for caring enough to say, "No spoilers, dear God, no more spoilers." Thank you, Angela Kang, for the future and beyond. Thank you, Greg Nicotero, for making the zombies (er, walkers) REAL. Thank you, Chris Hardwick, for telling the world every week that there's a comic book worth checking out. Thank you to the ten thousand people who work on the now FOUR TV shows based on THE WALKING DEAD for pouring their hearts into this and loving this world as much if not more than I do.

But most of all, thank you, Charlie Adlard, for sitting at the table, day in and day out, and devoting more hours to THE WALKING DEAD than anyone. I couldn't have asked for a better partner. It's been a dream come true to get to shape this world together, with you. This never would have happened without you. I can't believe we made it all the way to the end, my friend.

Oh my god... I can't believe it's really over.

-Robert Kirkman

P.S. Negan Lives.